Joseph Kindon

Poems and Dramatic Sketches

Joseph Kindon

Poems and Dramatic Sketches

ISBN/EAN: 9783337158316

Printed in Europe, USA, Canada, Australia, Japan

Cover: Foto ©Andreas Hilbeck / pixelio.de

More available books at **www.hansebooks.com**

POEMS

AND

DRAMATIC SKETCHES.

BY

JOSEPH KINDON, B.A.

London:

NEWMAN & CO.,

43, HART STREET, OXFORD STREET, W.C.

1879.

PREFACE.

I PUBLISH this volume of my poems with a mixture of diffidence and confidence. It is the first venture of the kind I ever made; so that I have no experience of what may suit the public taste. I am inclined to suspect that my style and ideas, because they are so different from those of the poets of the day, are little likely to win admirers. These children of my imagination have been brought up in home seclusion, and are now going amongst strangers. What wonder, then, if the graces which the father saw in them should disappear when they come under entirely impartial eyes? At the same time, I feel that a father, who has employed the best years of his life and much serious thought in training his children, may fairly expect they will succeed when he sends them into the world with the blessing of God invoked upon them. To drop metaphor : it is not for the poet to criticise, and a perfectly unbiassed judgment on his own works is least of all to be expected of a man glowing with creative imagination ; it is for the poet to produce, and to have as little of the negative faculty about him as is consistent with exact and clear expression. If any one doubts, from my poetry, whether I have this claim to creative imagination, I myself have so little doubt of its possession that I make it my defence for publishing this book.

A few words as to the dramatic sketches which take up most of the volume. They have appeared in this form only for convenience. That is, it is not pretended that they display any stage-constructiveness, or could possibly be acted; but where the interest turns on character, a dramatic form is obviously an advantage ; it abridges description and raises a gently harmonious illusion in the mind of the reader. My idea has been to appeal to the great majority of educated people, who do not go to theatres. I have thought they would probably welcome interesting exhibitions of character in a dramatic form.

INDEX.

———

MORAL POEMS.

SACRED POEMS.

DRAMATIC SKETCHES.

POEMS.

A POET'S CREED.

THE summer evening glory shone,
And round the glowing sun's bright throne
   Hung roseate clouds ;
Fresh cooling airs from earth arose,
And wakened birds from their repose
   In leafy shrouds.

I wandered on I scarce knew where,
And sought in peaceful evening air
   A calm I wanted ;
With yet a lingering hope to find
Some secret sympathy by kind
   Sweet nature granted.

Ere this I had found might and power
Sweep with her winds, with thunder lower,
   Soar from her ocean,
Around me like a sea outspread,
From many a riven mountain-head,
   Stopped in wild motion.

B

But oftener would some gentler spell
Disorded joy or sorrow quell—
            A flower's grace,
The tint of cloud, the song of birds,
The pine-wood that speaks more than words,
            And takes thought's place.

And now my heart sank for the voice
With which sweet mothers bid rejoice
            Despairing ones ;
My hopes were gone, my prospects fled,
And all the blame upon my head
            That they throve once.

Once, but for doltish indolence,
Or other rarer gifts' pretence,
            I had been learned ;
A treasure-house of ancient lore,
Filled with sweet wisdom all before
            By glad toil earned.

Once (I had far gone on the road)
I might with skill have eased the load,
            Sickness and pain
Has laid on fellow-mortals here ;
But bade them scarcely with a tear
            To others 'plain.

It was their duty : I could plead,
Mine was to write what men would read
        Ages to come ;
Bright fame would crown me, I should know
The poet's fire, its glory throw
        Around my home.

How often words like genius, fame,
Have tempted fools their lot to blame,
        To scorn their sphere ;
And leaving useful tasks, to try
The path that their mad vanity
        Alone thinks clear.

These thoughts for long my brain had kept,
And paced with me as on I stept,
        My eyes on earth ;
At last when far from any town,
I looked to see if there was shown
        Aught seeing worth.

My lane had led me to a gate,
Through which great pleasure seemed t'await
        The wandering feet ;
With softest green the eye was cheered ;
Around protecting hills upreared,
        With smiles did greet.

I sat and gazed upon their smiling,
And soon my frowns ceased at their wiling ;
   By soft airs fanned,
I closed my eyes, and drearily
My old thoughts paced on wearily,
   Like feet on sand.

But now, as in some changing dream,
New objects came with sudden gleam,
   And thoughts akin :
One brightest form chased every shade,
And thoughts attendant stately played
   Their gladder sheen.

I thought that from these hills a Grace,
Slow as a summer cloud swims space,
   Down stepped to where
I gazing sat ; her form was one
That wingless like an angel's shone
   With colours fair.

With graceful, meditative motion
She crossed the sward like rays o'er ocean—
   Downcast her eyes,
As if she listened to the airs
That breathed above, from unseen players
   Soft melodies.

Round her the lightest robes were trailing,
Her beauteous-moulded limbs scarce veiling;
          A moon 'midst cloud!—
Her arms, and feet, and ankles bare
Showed in their curves and outlines rare
          A beauty proud.

She nearer drew, and her sweet face
Was radiant, smiling with the grace
          Of sweetest thinking;
But oh! the stately symmetry
Which triumphed there abashed my eye
          From her lids shrinking.

Upon her rainbow-robes I saw
Pictures, not such as painters draw—
          Art's wondering pride;
But such as nature's that are brought
On sunny tables—mirror-caught,
          Rich country side.

And as she nearer came I traced
Familiar spots, scenes such as graced
          Our English isle:
Fair Devon's vales, the lakes and hills
Of Westmoreland—farms, meadows, rills'
          Sweet English smile.

Here rivers rolled by many a town ;
There castled heights the woodlands crown ;
　　　　　There wide moors lay ;
While bare and craggy round the coasts,
Huge bouldered rocks held foaming hosts
　　　　　Of waves at bay.

Then forms of men appeared ; and bore
Their painted stature on to war ;
　　　　　Tall, stalwart braves !
With scythéd chariots, slings and bows,
The mailed firm Romans to oppose—
　　　　　Machine-drilled slaves !

And one supreme, Caractacus,
Fought with the foremost ; yet ev'n thus
　　　　　Defied steel-thrusts ;
He broke the phalanx :—one form too,
A woman's, with Iceni few
　　　　　But valour trusts.

There was the king—that age's boast,
Fighting sea-robbers' myriad host ;
　　　　　Then wise as brave,
Bidding just laws and learning's light
Found for all time strong England's might
　　　　　O'er land and wave.

A brave successor, in whose veins
The same wise courage ran, there strains
        With treacherous friends
Against a stronger foe ; he falls—
Then Freedom leaves her desolate walls ;
        His soul attends.

The lion-hearted monarch's force
Here marshals 'neath the sacred cross,
        And fills the strand ;
There the great conqueror brave harangues
The Crécy-famed, each bow-string twangs,
        Swords wave in hand.

One royal speaker more did give
Thought to each face in crowds, made live
        War-gesture wild—
A queen who sent few ships to brave
The mighty world-rich fleet and save
        Freedom's rule mild.

By her rule saved was the slight seed
Of native culture and the creed
        Of bold hearts true ;
Great Shakspeare, Bacon, Hooker then
Wrote from free child-heart o'er again
        What strong brains knew.

I saw where counsellors were met
To drive a tyrant off, and set
                    The greatness proved
On throne, where aye sat sire and son,
Changed but by death—they braved this wrong
                    Who freedom loved.

Lo! there the tide of anarchy
Beat on our coasts, and liberty
                    Swooned in death-fear;
Ev'n Pitt was changing hue, but spoke
The calm wise faith that ever broke
                    Thought's chain and spear.

These scenes for long my eyes delayed,
At length I glanced at her afraid
                    Of rude surprise;
But she with lids like dawning's mist
Rising that eastern light has kissed,
                    Smiled in my eyes.

I stood to hear her reverently,
Scarce daring yet to lift my eye
                    To her grand face;
But still I watched that moving scene
That on her robe was to be seen:
                    Miles in that space!

I heard her voice melodious say :
'All hail, my bard, that on this day
        I come to meet ;
In me this England's Muse regard ;
I come to show thy fate's not hard,
        That fair hopes greet.

'Know, that upon this English land
I long have dwelt with my sweet band
        Of fairy Graces.
Since the third Edward's reign our tongue
Began to mould, is shown in song
        My spirit's traces ;

' No other land but this blest isle
Has shone so 'neath a Muse's smile ;
        Its second sun !
Awaking strains in every age
That like her sweet birds' throw the gage
        To all lands down.

' There never have been wanting long
Some to take up this deathless song ;
        I now prompt those
Whom Fame rewards for sweetest lays
Such as these more inglorious days
        Can never lose.

'But most are scornful of their day,
And many heedless what I say
                        To prompt their tongue,
Who sweeping with long skill the chords
Lose heart, and pale their glowing words
                        Lore's ashes 'mong;

'Yet spite of all this seeming strife
'Tween this age and the poet's life,
                        My kingdom lasts.
Long as this earth shall change her seasons,
Beauty, in spite of poets' treasons,
                        The soul repasts.

'Though chiefly through my sweet bards' singing
I send each rapt heart heavenward winging;
                        Yet with my wand
I can my spirits bid to touch
With solemn joy the heart of such
                        As gazing stand.

'To thee I come that thou may'st know
Thou hast in power to bestow
                        Great boon on many.
I give thee here of my choice spirit;
But let it be thy next-best merit
                        To sing to any.

' Oh, scorn not thou in times like these,
When wealth is chased and then dull ease,
To sing aloud
Of simple tastes and labours mild ;
Believe the fresh heart of a child
'Neath the most proud.

' Go, like sweet Burns, to every heart
Without the trills and turns of art ;
And sing thy strain,
Wildly and free as Chaucer's rhyme
Rings down the avenues of time,
And charms world-pain.

' Thou canst not match these glorious two ;
Yet follow after, with as few
Deep heart-felt words.
And eyes will bless thee though unseen,
And hearts awake that dead have been,
With trembling chords.

' I've watched thee when thou wouldst resign
Thy hated task, the poet's line
To pore upon ;
I wept that beauty's votary
With grim disease at war should sigh
For sweetness flown.

'Yet would thy mind become a mansion
In which thoughts feasted—'neath th' expansion
              Of sunny heaven.
How often have my spirits hasted
To add new flame to feeling wasted
                    By some pang given.

'I stood by thee in foreign land—
Think ! when thy pleased eye did command
              Moselle's fair vale :
Think of that spring on thy return
When with this land's grace thou didst burn,
                    That flushed words pale ;

'And when to Learning's noble home
Thou like an uncaged bird didst come,
              I still stood by ;
And reverence for the 'mighty dead '
Ne'er scorched the dew my spirits shed,
                    Nor thralled thine eye.

'But oft thy heart glowed with my fire
Whilst wandering past each lovely spire,
              Each stately building ;
Where Architecture's majesties
Are retinued by memories—
                    Clouds of sun's gilding !

' I and my spirits gave yet more—
To glow with love, and to adore
                    That fair sweet girl ;
And when the beauty of her face
Had pierced thy heart, we calmed the pace
                    Of its mad whirl.

' I touched thine eye to see her charm,
And with her grace thy heart did warm ;
                    Then whispering,
I gave sweet words and eloquence
To soothe strong passion's vehemence,
                    And raise its wing.

' Now long since it has been a flight
Above this world, a heavenly light
                    That cheers and guides,
Clouded but never quenched, and sure
To lead to her in that home pure
                    Where love resides.

' Then think of all I've given and give—
Choicest spirit with thee to live,
                    To few e'er given ;
Thou nevermore my form shalt see,
But while thou liv'st I leave not thee
                    Till by thee driven.

'Remember what I earlier said '—
With that a harp to hers was led
                    By unseen hand—
'Listen, and imitate this strain
So tender-wild, so sweetly plain—
                    'Tis my command!'

She sang and harped so solemnly,
It was a song so sweet and high,
                    That her robe's hem
I sprang to kiss; but on my sight
The stars shone out, and silent night
                    Stretched under them.

I called again and yet again—
'Return, great fairy, who dost deign
                    My griefs to cheer!
Oh, leave me not; thy words were sweet;
Again that melody repeat,
                    And singing clear.'

In vain! dark silence chilled my heart;
But long, reluctant to depart,
                    I often turned,
And light seemed oft my eyes to fill,
And once that song my heart to thrill,
                    For which I yearned.

SONNETS AND POEMS TO E. H.

I.

THOU, that with a soul as pure as radiant skies
  Of early morning turnest to high heaven
Looks with an angel's rapture glowing, eyes
  To which a more than earthly light is given :
Thou, with soft-parted lips that gently flutter
  In heart's response, slow waving like the leaves
Of a rich breathing rose, the words they utter
  Waked by a zephyr from heaven, that receives
The fragrance of thy saintly adoration,
  And to the throne from whence on errand great
It came, now wafts the incense-sweet oblation,
  And noblest gift earth can to heaven translate :
Pray too for me ; thy spirit soars above ;
But I can only crave for earthly love.

II.

I toil to reach a glorious, golden fleece,
  Having no store of wealth, no skill, no strength,
Unheeding weakness, watchfulness' decrease,
  The stormy voyage and its dreary length.

Thou far above me shinest as a sun
  To which I soar with feeble wings and flight.
Ah! distant goal to which I cannot run!
  Thou vanishing sweet dream of real delight!
Raised by an honoured father, great and good,
  Whose rank and honour lingers still to bless,
And deck thy gifts with honouring friends who stood
  Around him, and now guard thy happiness:
What can I say to give hope living breath?—
That ranks are levelled by strong love and death.

III.

How many Aprils has this old earth seen!
  What generations have spring's coming hailed!
The lives of all have like an April been,
  And each seems but one day to have prevailed;
Yet love that comes a lovely guest from heaven
  Has ever mocked at time and out-dared death;
To weary hearts such founts of glad youth given,
  That age seems breathing quick fresh youthful
    breath—
Oh then, dear love, what angel-power's in thee
  To change this life from death and pilgrimage
To what it has been, may for ever be,
  Part of eternal life upon earth's stage.
Alas! without thee I still wander on,
And shuddering think on generations gone.

IV.

Some minds there are that choose sad lower spheres,
  That mingle with base minds and dwell with
    thoughts
As dark as foul, till dark the world appears;
  While nobler love religion's bright resorts.
This dome of sky sunlighted, this wide earth,
  Are for all souls a palace and a home,
Telling the humblest of their heavenly birth,
  Th' enslaved of custom bidding freely roam.
Thou art of those who soar, I hourly fall;
  How thy great presence shames the mind in me!
And how thou summonest my noblest all!
  Alas! thy absence brings back tyranny.
My comfort is thou never wilt divine
My depth, but lift me to that height of thine.

V.

How often have I seen in cages penned
  Free-hearted skylarks that to cloudless skies
Outstretch their yearning wings, from their breast
    send
  A mingling strain of grief and ecstasies;
The noble strength of lordly beasts I've viewed,
  Chafing with hurried pace its limits round;
And rock-proud eagles with a mien subdued

C

Flashing eye-glory which no sky could bound—
Alas! for nature's joys embittered so;
　　Yet how much sweet this leaves, the sweetest gone.
These creatures miss not joy like me, or know
　　The agony of love that meets with none.
Others may touch thy hand; thine eyes will give
Smiles to the sound would make my sick heart live.

VI.

Life is a laughter, then a bitter strife;
　　We toil till age, thence darken to the grave;
How weak society and vain its life!
　　Yet is wise solitude but sadly brave.
O poets sage and pastors, keep concealed
　　These truths, that they may taste but day by day.
What courage has one bright day's gleam revealed!
　　What hope when far clouds kissed religion's ray!
Poets are deaf to hope, and too much love
　　An earth where evil knowledge still does grow;
Their passion makes its bowers a wailing grove
　　That echo sunshine-joys, fulfilled hope's woe,
I am a singer too: love, think on me,
Trembling who brave impossibility.

VII.

The joyous birds ere gentle rain has ceased
    Sing out their gladness to the brightening sky;
And whom has not dull life awhile released
    Catching some picture or face-witchery?
How bright clear wit, great passion, a sad tale
    Can lift the burdened soul! Upon this earth
Sun-gladdened so, should thoughts immortal fail,
    One heaven-inspired would weigh the sun's high
        worth.
To-day 'twas more to me than sun or thought,
    Than to sweet birds returning sunny gleams—
Thou gavest friends what my heart eager caught,
    The smiles of sweet child-lips, eye-laughing beams :
Thy spendthrift friends take many such sweet gifts,
This hoarded theft my heart o'er all theirs lifts.

VIII.

Here where religion's awful spirit dwells,
    Hallowing the fane by heav'n-taught genius raised,
Prompting to lofty praise each breast that swells
    In transport, where adoring ages praised ;
Here where sad solemn sculptures point and speak
    Dumbly of him or her long lost to earth ;
But speaking trumpet-like—earth's hopes how weak !—
    Daily in prayer abasest thou thy worth.

Yet think not of poor human love as sin,
  Though sorrow pleads and heaven must be won ;
Think of it as a resting-stage souls win,
  A light in absence of religion's sun :
The soul has duties here ; its home's on high ;
Love is its life to all eternity.

IX.

Thou sweetest fair, the bloom of childhood still
  Flushes thy cheek ; a child's heart beats beneath
Thy tender bosom, womanhood does fill
  Thy dawning sky with beams that gild the wreath—
And shall I ask to lay upon thy heart
  My years of care and a thought-heavy head ?
Oh, think but this, sweet, life's years are no part
  Of cycles, centuries and eras fled.
To many life is but a hurried day—
  Place, wealth, fame, hide the splendour of the sun ;
But others storing beauty with time stray ;
  While poets gaze on and are ever young.
No burdens but fresh flowers my mind brings
To add to thine to which the dew yet clings.

X.

Sick for thy dearest love, how longing faints !
  Call it not madness, O ye mockers, nor
The poor conceit of folly ; for restraints
  It bows to ; pride such wounds of grief ne'er bore.

I weak among the strong with patience see
　All others cut their course through wind and wave,
Mourning that strength from fate should not quite flee,
　But sink to weakness, equalled by the grave—
Come, ye sunlighted lands, thou depth of sky,
　Tell me of strength and hope to outlive death,
Lend me your power, your grace, your mystery,
　Oh! let my soul on earth breathe native breath.
But for thy love—tears and entreaties blend,
That losing it too wretched life may end.

XI.

O sweetest of all England's sweet girl-faces!
　O spirit beauty come from heaven to earth!
Soft blended hues, most delicate form that graces
　Thought and true feeling and sweet woman-worth;
Since that glad day that first my happy eyes
　Blessed with thy vision true, as true as bright,
Thought has shone rainbow-hued, sweet melodies
　Has feeling tuned to ever new delight.
Dear girl, if ever on these words thou look,
　Frown not on praise of beauty never known,
Know that my heart the tears of April took
　To see a glory earth had never shown.
Hearts are immortal, and love not as eyes
In kindred-spirit all their beauty lies.

XII.

What is the solitude of desert wastes ;
  What the wild stormy breadth of darkened seas ;
To loneliness of heart when life distastes ;
  When dark around bids the soul's fears increase ?
How the companions of this earthly toil
  But mock our forms, remaining ghosts of men !
They have their griefs and joys, but hearts recoil,
  They altered not when your heart sank again.
What wretched strife, what fearful dread you've known ;
  And how again in terror you may stand.
Is life as ever by the future shown
  All stormy surges, with no pleasant land ?
No : heavenly love can guide and sweetly cheer—
God's can cast death's out, thine can quell life's fear.

XIII.

Alas ! for all mechanic toilers, for
  Noon-strength eclipsed, for lives that fade away.
Can hope and inward vision such restore
  To gladness, show a brighter dawning day ?
So the Book teaches, so this earth of ours
  Proclaims through all the gloom of wintry days ;
The grass remains and through the leafless bowers
  The thrush and robin hail the sun's weak rays.

But I'm no toiler; I am slave to naught,
    And call I heaven to bless as much again?
To enrich feeling, to ennoble thought?
    To give thy beauty happy arms to strain?
I ask, but claim not what's earth's joy above,
And limit judgment nor Almighty love.

XIV.

Such painful toil is here; this earth's a stage
    Set forth amid eternal time and space;
Passions inflame, lusts and ambitions rage,
    Invading all and each succeeding race.
And still insensible to love or strife
    The earth her seasons and her fruits renews;
It smiled when kings' ambitions poured out life,
    And no man but the greatest mourned to lose.
Can we then idly love, be mockers too,
    And laugh unsympathising in mad joy?
Yes: if no pride keep feeling sweet and true,
    And burning trial need search out no alloy.
The butterfly sips flowers all his day,
Yet on his wings the hues of heaven play.

XV.

Farewell—ah! what a doom lies in that word
    By our own lips pronounced; that word half-friends
Care not to speak; some little love is stored,
    Whose sunshine with that chilling shadow blends.

Oh, then what gloom's on me, who saw thy light,
   While hope grew stronger, who have felt the beams
Thy grace and beauty poured upon my sight,
   And now must see it but in shadowy dreams.
Scarce heard thy voice, not once I've touched thy
     hand;
   Then absence will be darkness; thou hast shared
Not one love-look, or word, or touch of hand
   To me, when my eyes all love's meaning dared.
' Farewell ' my breast heaves forth with deadly groan,
Farewell!   I wander heart-sick and alone.

XVI.

Once more to this thy city have I come:
   Thine ! for thou art the fairy of its streets;
And where thou smilest it is sunshine's home,
   Thy steps make music which thy speech repeats.
Oh, how the hot tears spring to my drooped eyes;
   Hardly I dare look where thy beauty shines—
It can so beam forth, wake such ecstasies,
   Or turned to wrath, be in me burning mines.
Longing to meet thine eye, what sickening fear
   Grasps at my hurrying heart lest what I writ
Call up a frown my yearning eyes to sear,
   My soul to pang as 'twould its mansion quit.
Oh ! look not so, great fairy, smile on me,
And let me truth for fevered vision see !

XVII.

I walked through fields to-day bright with the sun,
   And heard the joyous lark pour forth his glee;
Freshly the wheat's green pennons every one
   Waved, and the spring breeze wandered pleasantly—
Sunshine made all things glad : they mocked at him
   Who for more blessing than deep blue skies craved;
Whilst I walked spiritless, with vision dim,
   And with step heavy by the wheat that waved.
But thou wouldst pity wretchedness, who hast
   Such deep heart-reverence for sacred things,
And mingle tears of sympathy as fast
   As angel-raptures when the full choir sings.
Alas, what thoughts are these? it mocks distress
Thy gracious worth to know of, not possess.

XVIII.

Days come with promise to me; when they pass
   I'm to success no nearer; of each one
The sum is mere despair; as in a glass
   Faces, as trees in streams my hopes have gone.
The radiant visions were as ships in air,
   As oases to desert wand'rers, bliss,
Gleaned from out twenty lives and gathered there
   Where we two stood, light that both heads did kiss.

How then, what if this be so, man and child?
   This is full many a heart's awakening; thine
Is not more riven, not more desolate-wild,
   That felt love's transport answer gifts divine.
O cruel fair, though my love's scorned and spent,
My breast's no hell; God's love is given, not lent.

XIX.

O dearest, as a palely flushing bud,
   Dew-bright and shrinking, may-be virgin love
Starts to dream-beauty in thee, understood
   Best as a type of beauteous joys above!
Oh, if this greet hope's trembling, thank for me
   Him who has granted two hearts gladness to beam,
And tenderness unceasing; for to thee
   Life shall one interchange of dear love seem;
Bright will this sad earth be, although there come
   Sorrow and fierce temptation; yet if trust
Fail not in God's love and our own, the hum
   Of noon-day creatures born of the summer dust
Will be as misery to joy like ours,
Sown on this earth to bloom in heavenly bowers.

XX.

A feeble tongue have I to speak your praise;
   My verse is weak to glorify this theme;
Who that once heard thee, felt thy grace amaze
   His heart, would say I too had loved that dream?

Not this : ' Where are the golden gleams reflected,
   And rainbow hues in this dull stream of words? '
When my heart's finest strung the strain expected
   Comes by no touch æolian as to birds.
Why then do I invoke sweet poetry,
   And write, and strive with words, and cull the best?
That from chance-shifted words some witchery
   Your sweetest grace more nobly may attest.
Yet how can words with spirit-truth surprise
When hour-new thoughts of love for thee arise?

XXI.

Not for this life are raptures or despair ;
   Is it not written men may o'er-righteous be?
Nor can the soul (poor prisoner here) long stare
   On suns ideal from all earth-clouds free,
This know I ; so to keep the fountain pure
   Of love to thee which murmurs through my heart
I blend calm holy flowings with it, sure
   Peaceful-clear tides to torrents they impart.
Despair comes like a torrent : then I pray
   With tears to God which call down cheerful faith ;
But when thy beauty fond hope thinks to stay,
   Angelic peace is mine that knows not death.
Natures that sweet and holy are as thine
Always unconscious-sacred influence shine.

XXII.

What wilt thou write to me? thou art to write
Words I shall tremble to unseal, and read
With dim eyes and a beating heart, with white
And deathly face, a careless fatal speed.
It will be sweet denial—canst thou pray
For mercy, and to hope like mine a stern
And fearful death-blow deal?—No! thou wilt say
Kindly my doom, that I shall dimly learn,
Wilt write it with dim eyes; and I shall see
Through burning orbs its message, where a tear
Still stains the page; a sigh and fragrancy
Will float above my happiness' sad bier.
I will not say to hope, 'expect glad things,'
Thus murdering trust, bright as the lark that sings.

XXIII.

To-day I faced the pitiless rebuke
Of chill experience that age bestows
On summer-soft romance; my words and look
Glowed with its eloquence, then quickly froze—
Alas! the room I sat in must have seen
Often thy loveliness, have echoed to
Thy speech and laughter; here then I have been;
Here with strong passion I for thee did sue.

Nothing could move ; with trembling lips and speech
  Storm-eloquence broke from me ; from her came
Unruffled calm and wisest words ; with each
  She seemed to scorn my ' wrath of love ' to shame.
Then for a lip-white languor to control,
I summoned madness strength to fill my soul.

XXIV.

No longer will I pour out thought and verse
  To ease my heart, and thy great worth to prove ;
No words can utter it ; I'm tortured worse
  The more I whisper or groan forth my love—
Thou art so lovely pride were in good place ;
  So simple as no loveliness were there ;
So sweet and noble is thy mien and face,
  Rich thought and feeling too must be thy share.
I'd say with such a wealth of grace and gift
  Thou art an angel ; but thy womanhood
Is tender-gracious—oh, its traits uplift
  Thy love to angels, kind as sternly good.
Thou greatest heavenly blessing to a man,
I cannot match thee, but none other can.

THE
WORLDLY-WISE AND CUSTOM-CHILLED.

THE worldly-wise and custom-chilled
   Have ever railed on love like mine,
A world of duller forms has filled
   Their minds that never knew of thine,
Till all idea of such was killed.

And peace to them !—forgiveness for
   Their thrusting-stabs of wisdom, wit.
These earthly weapons cannot war
   'Gainst spirit, nor can hope to hit
Truth so beyond experience' lore.

Their prudent loves and social joy
   Are earth's rewards and labour's crown ;
The heaven that instincts here enjoy,
   Life's flower in country and in town,
Fairest when Death comes to destroy.

But can they know that there is love
   That flashed upon the eager soul
With light as from some star above—
   Though o'er it clouds for life must roll,
That fills for life the soul with love ?

They cannot—thou alone can'st guess,
　If burning words of anguish tell,
If gestures, acts are bars where press
　Souls passioning—the body's cell
As if to burst in their distress;

Then thou alone may'st antedate
　Th' eternal bloom my love shall know,
Thy dear love can alone abate
　The pangs of an immortal throe,
Which else must tardy Death await.

DULL CLOUDS MAY GLOOM.

Dull clouds may gloom the freshest green
　That decks the trees in gladdest May,
And thunder-showers the slender screen
　So pierce that drowned is the sweet lay
　　　　Rejoicing birds
Sang as if summer-eves had been,
　　　　And lovers' words.

Yet ere the setting of the sun
　The rain has ceased, the clustered leaves
A softer lustre have put on,
　While the still-listening air receives
　　　　The clear full notes,
Hailing gold-clouds as past each one
　　　　A cloud-veil floats.

Dear girl, thy beauty is more bright
　Than May and fresher than her leaf,
Thy graciousness—as winter's night
　Thy cloudy absence has to grief
　　　　Been and must be
Till more than summer bless my sight
　　　　In smiles from thee.

What music then would'st thou awake
In me who sing so feebly now !
How life itself would seem to make
A harmony that planets know;
        To music's laws
Bending its course; for thy sweet sake
        To glide or pause.

Oh, teach the worldly-wise who pour
Contempt when fondest lovers weep,
And teach the slave who would not war
A beauty in his heart to keep,
        That worth and grace
Answering to love like mine ask more
        Than this earth's space.

NO! NOT FOR ME THE LAY IS SUNG.

No! not for me the lay is sung ;
  No! not for me the jest is spoken ;
He cares not how my heart is wrung,
  He cares not how my spirit's broken.

I never meet his love-lit eye ;
  No sunny smile for me is beaming ;
He heeds not if I smile or sigh ;
  Nor knows that bitter tears are streaming.

He knows not—would he care to know ?
  Would even his triumph smile at seeing,
The agony of hopeless woe,
  The frenzy pale when life is fleeing ?

Why does he careless now neglect
  Her whose least sigh once wakened sorrow ?
Why did his tender looks reflect
  A beauty sunbeams cannot borrow ?

Awake, I pour despairing tears,
  Asleep, I dream of long past pleasure ;
Then gladly, Death, I'll meet thy fears.
  Oh, quickly bring oblivion's treasure.

N.B.—Only the last three quatrains are mine. The first
two are part of a song in three quatrains by Marian. I con-
sidered the last quatrain of this song so decidedly inferior to
the beauty of the preceding stanzas that I have ventured to
substitute some of my own composing.—J. K.

WHAT IS IT TO HAVE SEEN YOUR FACE.

WHAT is it to have seen your face,
   And to have known
Something of the enchanting grace
   Around you thrown ?

What is it to have seen you smile
   A lovely greeting ?
The face of each showing the while
   That hearts were meeting.

What is it to have seen you pray,
   And while the singing
Rose, to have watched the heavenly ray
   In your face springing ?

What is it to have known the grief
   Your absence brings ?
When blue skies, birds, field, flower and leaf
   Are joyless things.

What is it to have mourned in soul,
   When scorching tears
Chased one another, and the goal
   Friends hid with fears ?

When they and Prudence glanced at thee,
            Then cursed my folly;
Calling my true love-loyalty,
            Mad melancholy.

O fairest, sweetest all has been
            So bitter-sweet,
I could sad consolation glean
            Though ne'er we meet.

Bitter it is to have been near,
            But no word spoken;
Ne'er sunned on by your beauty clear
            In peace unbroken—

But to have known this earth can show
            A presence like thine,
Changes imagination's glow
            To hues divine;

And when such worth and holiness
            Has pierced the heart,
Thought has gained life and loveliness
            Unknown to Art.

To E. H.

AGAIN thou blessest these sad eyes
　　　That long have searched for thee,
And on the quiet minster lies
　　　Sweet awful mystery.

Thy face beams radiance ; the still air
　　　Seems fragrant—I can hear
Nought of the choir's praise, nought of prayer ;
　　　But floating music near.

I see thee only—thou art fair,
　　　And gracious as morning ;
I gaze as on sun-rising, where
　　　Birds hail day's returning.

A long night has thy absence been,
　　　I waked and wept in pain,
Groaning for what I once had seen
　　　That no day brought again.

Thou com'st once more, my joy, my life,
　　　My darkened soul's fair sun !
Oh, beam unclouded, end the strife
　　　By thy first sight begun.

Call me to thee with one kind smile
　　　　Then one sweet gracious word
Whisper—I shall look sad awhile,
　　　　Thinking it was not heard.

How mighty is thy power to bless;
　　　　I can scarce lower fall;
God can send woe or happiness—
　　　　Lord, unto Thee I call!

Spare this dear child of Thine the grief
　　　　I've known and yet may know;
Oh, let me ever in belief
　　　　Of loving-kindess glow!

IT MAY BE WE SHALL NEVER MEET.

IT may be we shall never meet
　　　　Again,
That ne'er shall kisses on thy sweet
　　　　Lips rain,

Nor thy quick-heaving bosom make
　　　　Mine glow,
Nor starting tears the lashes shake
　　　　Down slow ;

Silence will not be sweeter than
　　　　Our speech,
When the hushed breath and pulses can
　　　　Love teach.

Words will not linger that the eyes
　　　　May rove,
To tremors timed, as flushes rise,
　　　　To move.

Thy dear lips will not oracles
　　　　Reveal,
Sweet wisdom thought and sense each stills
　　　　To feel ;

For us romance in sunny bowers
  Is not,
Nor will enchantment twilight hours
  Allot.

If this be so a sigh shall be
  Each breath,
And with each wish that's born in me
  Call death ;

I will not rail on hope because
  She lied ;
Nor rage that Heaven's eternal laws
  So tried.

But with sad-patient eyes I'll view
  The past ;
Nor fear what coming false or true
  May haste ;

Only when others love I'll weep
  Awhile,
And when death's shadows o'er me creep
  Will smile.

DEAREST, LET INDIFFERENCE WEAVE.

DEAREST, let indifference weave
  Its moonlight grace
Around some other form, and leave
  For aye thy face.

Too long its marble stateliness
  Has clung to thee ;
It seems from veiling loveliness
  Lovely to be ;

But oh, how lovelier were thy brow
  In pity bending;
What tender grace thy laugh would show
  With my song blending.

Thou can'st more lovely be, sweet face,
  More stately-gracious,
Thou moving form with leaf-waving grace
  'Gainst blue heaven spacious !

How my poor heart felt ecstasy,
  Thinking it saw
Tremulous kindness glisten thine eye,
  And mine o'erawe.

If this was not seen; poor, poor heart!
And sadder life;
With some scenes wholly, all in part
Sick-desperate strife.

Dearest one, rouse me from sweet sad dreams
T, waking bliss,
Shine forth, let these be sunrise gleams
That thin clouds kiss;

Tell me I saw most true when light
Of love seemed breaking,
That my heart truly hailed the sight
As the lark earth forsaking.

Oh, how I then could sing to thee,
And live for ever,
Gazing on heart-felicity
Death could not sever!

Death comes to aged in heart and limb,
Not to pure-loyal
Souls that sing thanksgiving with eyes dim
For God's gift-royal.

SWEET IS YOUR FACE.

Sweet is your face—oh sweeter far
   Than thought can measure,
And genius must describing mar
   Your heart's rich treasure.

O misery! that such rich worth
   Of face and heart
Should sadden all this lovely earth,
   Soul-gloom impart!

That one should sigh for them and find
   They cannot be;
Another win careless as wind
   Their fragrancy.

Is this God's will lest such rich joys
   Should make earth, Heaven—
Is ecstasy and mid-sky poise
   But one bird given?

Must thou, sweet girl, with rich gifts bless
   One who them spurns,
Scarce glancing at the loveliness
   That my heart burns?

Oh, do not so !   Good God, avert
        This joyless wreck ;
Let not the unloving her desert
        And beauty deck !

But give them me—let order reign,
        And pleasure free,
In two lives pure from licence-stain,
        Find liberty.

SONG.

Come, brave mounting lark, O trill;
  Let me happy know
Where bright May flowers drink the rill,
  And its margin glow.

Summer-joy, O blackbird pipe,
  On glad echo call,
Till your notes crowd thick like ripe
  Fruit on orchard wall.

Thrill the heart of fragrant glooms,
  Nightingale, delay
Melody as light entombs
  Every starry ray.

Poet, let all grace o'erflow,
  Music, image pour,
Till thy page have caught the glow
  Heavenly fancy wore.

Long delayed, come victor Love,
  Bring one thought of her;
Nothing more than heaven above
  May excel that fair.

To E. H.

SOMETIMES to a lovely face
    Tenderly
Wanders, and in beauty's maze
    Dwells mine eye ;
But my heart is faithful to thy grace.

Often on my listening ear
    Falls a tone
Light and laughing, sweet and clear,
    Girlhood's own ;
And I smile to think that thou art near.

Rarely comes a grace of motion
    From afar,
And my heart beats with devotion ;
    Yet at war
Thinks of thee with tenderer emotion.

Never beauty, sweetness, grace,
    Like to thine,
Could I in another trace—
    Heart of mine !
Though alone each seems to take thy place.

Visit oft my mind and wake
    Ecstasy.
Oh, thy mien and voice will make
    Ear and eye
Dream and fairest presences forsake.

FRIENDS WHO BID ME.

FRIENDS who bid me banish thee,
   Banish thee from all my thoughts,
Can they guess the secrecy,
   Secrecy of love's resorts,
When new love for thee is found
In each lovely sight and sound?

They who talk of wretchedness,
   Wretchedness of hopeless love,
Can they deem this weariness,
   Weariness their peace above,
When I who could never get
Word or look can ne'er forget?

They who speak of happiness,
   Happiness apart from thee,
Can they know the dreariness,
   Dreariness of life to me.
When thy beauty blessed my eye
Was it beauty that could die?

They who hint at faithlessness,
　Faithlessness! If they can find
One of thy worth and graciousness,
　Graciousness might change my mind;
But they know not, as I know,
One like thee dwells not below.

Dearest, see my love and woe,
　Love and woe's fidelity,
Only thou canst ever know,
　Ever know my loyalty—
Must in my breast dumbly plead
Truth but thy love's truth can read?

EVENING.

The setting sun now leaves the sky,
  And tinges western clouds with glory;
The birds 'cross darkening heaven fly;
  The falling leaf tells winter's story;

The kine in distant meadows low;
  By fitful gusts the trees are driven;
Then silent gleams the moon, and slow,
  With stately step, she climbs the heaven;

The stars are following one by one;
  The crimson from the west is failing;
The moon has now the heavens won,
  And through bright clouds is proudly sailing.

I leave with steps unwilling, slow,
  Such glorious views of earth and heaven:
Ah, why should man so seldom know
  The peace, the love to Nature given!

SNOW-STORM.

Now Nature pours
Her fleecy stores
Wide over all the plain;
The mad wind shakes
The feath'ry flakes,
Dancing to sky again.

The blinding shower
Makes small birds cower,
And fly to cottage thatch;
Man shuns in haste
The stormy blast,
And presses down the latch.

Deep, deeper yet,
Her coverlet
Kind Nature lays on earth;
The wind may blow
His keenest now,
Young seeds will have their birth.

'Tis winter's smile
That doth beguile
The horrors of his reign:
Thus all the year
Does beauty cheer;
Till green Spring smiles again.

TO A SKYLARK.

Lark ! that wheeling in thy flight
Singest to the god of day,
Rising now with streaming light,
Scatt'ring eastern clouds away.

Thou the spirit of the scene,
Chasing envious clouds afar,
Soon as e'er his face was seen,
Sang'st his triumph in the war.

Else why to the earth so near
Circles thy impulsive flight ?
Who when heaven is blue and clear,
Soar'st beyond the reach of sight.

Hence thy song's impetuous thrill !
Hence thy wild, impulsive flight !
Victory thou dost herald shrill,
Gained by sun o'er clouds of night.

Bravest bird, that stay'st below,
When all heaven thou might'st enjoy :
Duty thus done, we should know,
P'r'aps thy ecstasy of joy.

TO A THRUSH SINGING AT DAYBREAK.

SWEET Thrush, that high upon a leafless tree
  With loud note hailest the scarce dawning east;
Fly not ! but still pour forth melody—
  Stay where the light shines on thy speckled breast.

Far up yon valley now in mist concealed,
  Thy notes came mingled with the gurgling stream,
Now loud, now faint, by distance half-revealed,
  They sounded sweet as in a pleasant dream.

Long hast thou sung and happy was thy strain
  While creeping fog hid all the earth from sight ;
But see ! at length the sun bursts forth again
  And silvers curling mists with shafts of light.

I came to thee with sorrow at my heart ;
  By hope deluded, sick of this world's strife—
Whether my fault or others caused the smart,
  I loved not man nor cared for my own life.

I looked on Nature with a careless eye,
  On melancholy preyed with brooding soul ;
In vain to me her hills, her fields, her sky
  In rich variety she did unroll.

But hearing thee—thou sing'st in very scorn
  Of unbelief and spite and bitter hate :
I everything forget whilst I am borne
  On floods of joy and love that ne'er abate.

Farewell, sweet bird ! 'midst roar of cities' strife,
  This song of thine shall sweeten memory ;
Through hardest years of aging, wearying life,
  My love shall childlike grow with thoughts of thee.

TO THE WIND AT MIDNIGHT.

Howl, thou Wind, o'er moor and ocean ;
  Sailor s wife and wanderer scare ;
Crash the trees ; let wave-commotion
  Darkening surge ; the moon's face bare !

Scream thy triumph, blusterer, soaring
  Where the clouds in quiet lie ;
Dive 'neath ocean, swell thy roaring
  With the thunder of the sky.

I can laugh at thee, this shelter
  Trembles not, though thou assail ;
Summon ice, thy fiercest pelter !
  Shield and sheltered never quail.

Friend !—a rough one ; I no longer
  Blame thy manners ; long I've known
Health thou giv'st, the more, the stronger
  Wings thy flight o'er sea and town.

I'll not call thy generous speeding
  Rough, unceremonious haste :
Perhaps to some sky-anthem's leading
  True's the voice howls o'er the waste.

TO TWO PRIMROSES IN EARLY MARCH.

O PALE twin sisters I could weep
Seeing how tremblingly you peep
   With sweet sad faces :
Alas ! the beams that wakened you
Should first have whispered, ' Weeks ensue
   Ere spring-time graces.'

Then ye had lien awhile, to spring
When violets have blossoming ;
   Ye would have gazed
On flowery banks and leafy trees,
To hear the lark's sky-ecstasies
   Your heads had raised.

Now ye must look on dull grass growing,
Now ye must feel the March winds blowing ;
   The clouds' dull rack
See drearily blue heaven pace,
Against them rustling branches trace
   All bare and black.

Ye cannot frown, ye came to show
Beauty, and kindness to bestow ;
   Frowned on austerely,
Ye can but plead, with tenderer look,
That ye were born in your dull nook
   To please it merely.

WRITTEN IN MARCH.

Upon this high rock seated, how mine eyes
Exult to view sunlighted moorland, far
Down-stretching miles cloud-shaded. Oh, ye clouds,
That high above me float—how are ye charmed!
How slowly do ye pace and earthwards gaze
Where your light shadows dance o'er the gold-brown
      heather.
O! ye soft breezes, how like spirits free,
Ye wave this tract, then rising fan my cheek,
Then pipe aloft your music! O fair earth,
O lands awaiting April's tears and laughter,
Though Spring be not yet come, yet fiercest Winter
With blasts, has left you smiling patiently!
Come ever thus to me, thus sweetly courted
By sunbeams, by the breezes and the clouds,
And I like thee will smile. For as to thee,
Though now 'tis early summer with me too,
Decay and grief will come, and wintry age,
If bright yet cold—a form that is less lovely,
Less patient than your own. Then visit me,
Me who now love thee carelessly, and like
A child its mother; me in whom the wealth
Of children, rich soul-sunshine, now may seem
By manhood but thin clouded; when I laugh

At shallow laughter, and thy quiet smile
Appears a sweet rebuke—come to me thus,
In watchings, amid losses, in the dreams
Of age's night, and sunny gratitude
Shall beam from me too—thanksgiving to God,
And to friends ministering tenderness,
A sunset glow and harvest of sweet smiles,
So heart-felt, so ennobling those dull clouds
That throng my setting, and so breaking through,
With such quick following streams of golden light,
That it shall overflow the fountain even
Of their soul-beauty ; those who came denyingly
Shall find in charity its own reward,
And solace treasured for much future toil,
Less gracious perhaps, less pitying than this
Lavished on me, for sweetness that was thine.

TO BIRDS SINGING IN THE END OF FEBRUARY.

WHAT calls your chanting forth, sweet birds—
    Bare trees? a leaden sky?
A month of piercing winds ere Spring
    Deck your homes daintily?

Or does this dull still evening smile?
    That hill-side stand out clear?
Its hanging woods, are fragrant shades
    And lovely hues yet there?

The western glory, is it gone?
    Was earth a lovely sky?
Have odorous gales scarce seemed to breathe,
    And then swept sighing by?

Or did your little tender mates
    Ask for some solace sweet?
And do you, stifling coward-fears,
    With promises them greet?

Yes, you are saying, ' Wait, sweet wife,
    Green shall your bower be ;
The wind you feared so yesterday
    Shakes not a leafy tree.

'Think, when the sunbeams dance, and I
　　Swing by your side as gay;
The breeze that brings the sunbeams tuned
　　By leaves to my sweet lay.

' Then will this bare cold earth provide
　　Sweet fruits and many a flower;
Then will we bring our little ones
　　Some fresh food every hour.'

Blest are poor birds who dream this dream,
　　Compared with yonder man :—
We realize as much again;
　　Their dreams exceed life's span.

ADDRESS TO THE COUNTRY ON A RETURN TO IT AFTER LIVING IN LONDON.

Once more I greet you, hills and plains and fields,
Wide stretching skies and winds that freely roam,
Hail to you all ! Ye too, still dearer friends,
Green tender things, high branching trees, sweet
    flowers,
And every singing, every flying bird !
How happily your freedom once again
My spirit tastes. Oh, how your innocent ways
And buoyant gestures make it dance again
To your own long-loved measure ! I for long
Was prisoned in a city ; nothing there
Could cheer my heart like one brief glance of love
In your sweet faces. Beauty lives not there,
And money cannot bring it to the streets
That Commerce throngs. I've gazed on all wealth's
    glitter,
Then sighed for gentleness like yours ; have yearned
For nobly-simple liberty like yours,
Then said it must be there—it was not there
Although 'twas sky above and earth below.
I shuddered meeting day by day but crowds,
    ot men, but forms enslaved, all meeting crowds,

And crowds still hurrying, following after crowds.
But you refresh me! I will think those weeks
A wicked dream of weeks—let me forget it!
Speak to me, sunny hills, where shadows dance,
And utter solemn music, sweeping winds;
Roll in your grandeur, clouds that pace heaven's blue,
And speak with majesty to humblest things;
Awe with your thunder, flee through space, or pause
Glancing your shafts of light, while man's heart
    speaks.
Ye waving trees, fresh green things, little birds,
Commune again as ever delicately
With kindred graces, or us fellow-mortals.
Prompt me each day to mingle with your beauties,
Your thousand kindnesses, my sweetest fancies,
Clear faith and hope, contentment, liberty,
Unenvying charity, and gratitude.
This interchange be ours till death shall come;
Then may I gently die like one of you,
Leaving a fragrant memory on earth,
Unsorrowing beauty, love that cannot die.

TO EVENING CLOUDS.

Ye clouds that softly glow in the western sky,
Ye gentle hills, fairer than earth can show,
With what calm grace ye float, and pause to dream
Where tender blue is fading ! Ye are as bowers,
As happy Eden-homes for blest-sweet spirits
To dwell in, gazing on your love and beauty ;
And yet themselves more loving-beautiful,
Wiser than thought or speech, and raying goodness.
My soul was as a weary sun-scorched stream
Hidden 'midst rocks, faint as the sheltering birds,
Or as a flower whose petals thirst for dew,
With thoughts of earth clogg'd as by frost is lock'd
The liquid music in the song-birds' throats.
But ye have beamed in beauty, like the smiles
Of bride or mother, calling gladness forth,
Bidding soul-freedom cheerfully to live—
As you glide on desponding not, with grace
Answering the louder triumphs of the day,
And not despairing though dull night, and then
A day's glare, intercept the evening hours.
And shall my soul, whose nobler beauty can
Far oftener shine, ev'n here on earth, where passion
Proclaims herself divine, and senses claim
All strength—shall it not speak authority ?

And with a silent eloquence o'erwhelming ?
Since an eternal sunshine is its home;
A king himself, love, beauty, goodness, truth,
Will give its gazing rapture faculties,
With worlds of beauty, graces, and rich pomps
Attendant like to yours and far surpassing.

LINES ON THE POET COWPER.

GREAT Christian-poet, glory of our land,
Worthy successor of the prophet-band,
Whose numbers less from human genius flow
Than with the Spirit's aid divinely glow !
How shall I justly praise unfailing skill,
Themes which themselves our soul and reason fill ;
And modesty and goodness that appear
Attendant wit and transport high to fear !
Great poet and great Christian, what but grace
Could change the course that Pride bade Genius
    trace ?
Who save great David or Isaiah yet
Strove not beyond success or truth to get ?
Who in these flowery paths would rest content
With here and there a pretty wild-flower's scent ?—
Only the less by all the Muses fired
Than by the word of God himself inspired !
And thou art of the glorious few, howe'er
Thy earthly life showed desolate and bare,
Thine was the gloom (none such before or since)
A palace-solitude might yield a prince ;
A two-fold grandeur, intellectual light
And spirituality—a snow-capped height !
None of the ' mighty dead ' could sympathise,

F

Nor any living feel thy ecstasies;
Only on consecrated Bible-ground
Awful and fit companionship was found.
Ye poets greater far in taste's esteem,
Compared with his what must your laurels seem?
Rewards vain intellect for flattery gives,
For incense by which false refinement lives.
Here yield your titles to whose lesser name
Felt all your fires, but never stooped to fame;
Could swell with ardour, yet with grace retire
From turgid pomp and passion some call fire;
His wit and delicatest humour play,
Yet idiot-sprightly licence spurn away.
Which of you would have dared to choose your
    themes,
Or fashion them alone where Heaven's light beams?
Where then had been your volumes, where your
    praise
Outlasting life, to endure immortal days?—
There had your pages lived and there your fame,
With his, unquenched by all the last day's flame,
Echoed perhaps above in angel-strains,
A lofty song of truth that aye remains.

REVERENCE.

'That angel of the world.'—(SHAKSPEARE.)

IF seeking knowledge we miss reverence,
Then all our knowledge is a fair pretence ;
Knowledge gives sight and skill for earth's rewards ;
Her eyes and wings can raise us heavenwards :
The poorest man and duller than the clods,
In pagan times, she made the friend of gods :
Since God no more to walk with man descends,
She is the trusted messsenger He sends :
To vassal man since closed was Eden's door,
She comes from God's high court th' ambassador.
The charter of our heavenly liberties
Is writ in language known but to her eyes ;
And of God's speech, unlearned since man's offence,
The kind interpreter is Reverence.

PLEASURE.

Pleasure, best loved friend of man !
Sought by him through all life's span,
Hast thou had in heaven thy birth,
Worshipped as thou art on earth ;
Man and woman, rich and poor,
Thou dost to thy shrine allure ;
And receiv'st their richest treasure,
Hard-earned gains and scanty leisure ;
Money, health, time, thought is given
To enjoy thy earthly heaven ;
Wise, fool, knave, thy votaries,
Cynics, who deem all else lies.
Toilers brain and body tasking
Are but deeper motive masking ;
And when most in drudgeries mixt
Most on thee their eyes are fixt :
Pleasure ! dost thou will disarm ;
If not, say what is thy charm ?
Poet, who dost now inquire
Why all men me so desire ;
Who although a favourite
Canst not fathom with thy wit
What should be my subtle charm,
With which man's will I disarm.

Knowledge⁻on thee I now bestow;
Poets and children best I know ;
And when knowledge too is thine
Teach thou those who me malign :
Few but seeking me find care ;
All the world my seekers are ;
Those who find me but a name
Now I'll show themselves must blame.

See, first my loveliest votaries !
Who throng the palace rooms,
And through the long night's glooms
Shine on each heart with sweet words and eyes ;
Through long lighted chambers gay music sounds,
And lightly the foot of each dancer bounds :
Friendship and love join hands ;
Beauty to grandeur lends her grace ;
Formality unbends, to give mirth place ;
Who with the hard-won triumph flushed each heart
    commands.

The crowded theatre next view,
Where words of genius ever new
The fate of gods, and heroes great unroll,
See, how the graceful gesture, well-formed speech
Sway the passion-pierced soul !
The mind's feast share to ear and eye ;
While eloquence and wisest maxim teach,
    And dwell for ever in the memory :

The heroes' language learnt, all march toward heroes'
    goal.
But ecstasy soon falls below the height I reach.

See laughing comedies revealing
    The age's follies—each one clearly showing;
But with bright wit the worst concealing;
    While frowns are changed to looks with red mirth
        glowing.

Hark! how the lofty hall resounds
    To silent multitudes,
Where choral singing joined to harmonies
Of instruments, from walls and roof rebounds;
    Then ceases; desert solitudes
Are like the place, whilst one short moment lies
A rapture on the heart past utterance;
    Long afterwards does memory
    Flutter the heart with joy, brighten the eye
With what was heard and felt as in a trance—
Seeming a foretaste, echo perhaps of heavenly
    symphonies.

Long could I speak of this; but lo!
My name is called by different earth-dwellers—
    The midnight riotous care-quellers,
The debauchee, the drunkard—all who know
    Fierce joy when quiver tongues and reel the
        brains;

When headstrong degradation
Is blown to a flame by emulation ;
And he is best fool-knave whom worst crime stains ;
The wisest who has worst life seen and known ;
The wittiest whose thoughts' clothes
Are the most blasphemous oaths ;   [groan.
While judgment exiled sits and murdered feelings

Now, see my kingdom where I'm absolute ;
The chambers of young childhood's breast are
mine ;
No rival there intrudes, fierce joy to scorn
Our happiness ; with dazzling shine
To turn our fresh shade to a desert bare ;
No tiger-malice from him born ;
That having tasted once mad licence-fare
With craving never satisfied is cursed ;
But sets revenge to waste, and ev'ry flower uproot.
Far different they—the sight of butterfly
Or bird can make their bubble-envies burst :
Such joys are not so loud,
But that their hearts can sing reply ;
Nor so outshining that through slumber's shroud
In dreams returning they the lightest sleep outstare.

One other kingdom holds my sway,
Not absolute, as childhood's, yet
A sister-kingdom there is set ;
With poets and the lovers of their art,

The humble wooers of great Nature's grace,
To whom she gives her power to sway the heart,
   The gentle beauty that each draws ;
   The might of law that overawes ;
Her shapes and colours make thought's living face :
The heart of man to this sweet influence gives
Its secrets, like an air-harp changing,
As kindred winds are o'er it ranging :
'Tis thus fair truth with beauty lives
In every age's verse ; and where these come I stay.

FOURTH SUNDAY IN LENT.

Shut from Thy presence, Lord, cast from Thy love,
This is on earth to lose Heaven above ;
'Lone with my sin and its bondage to dwell,
This is in life to be living in hell.
Oh, give me not wealth, give not wealth's pleasures
    here,
Bestow not sweet fame or the world's titles dear ;
Let no woman's love, no sweet converse be mine,
Let intellect, wit, or sweet fancy ne'er shine ;
Nature's beauties or grandeurs ne'er gladden my heart,
Nor taste and refinement delight me in Art—
But raise me once more to communion with Thee,
Make sin's beauty hateful and thus make me free,
Confessing my vileness, not cherishing sin.
Oh ! cause Truth's bright dawning on night to begin,
Then hideous spectres shall vanish away,
And passion's wind cease with the brightness of day ;
Thy word will have calmed the tempestuous wave
And I shall be nearer my port in the grave.

FIFTH SUNDAY IN LENT.

LORD, while on Thee I trust
  How am I blest!—
This world's a sinful maze,
  Long since I must
Have perished, or been wandering ill at rest,
  Did not Thy love
Watch with such tenderness my ways,
  That where I dangers pass
I sternly eye with courage from above
  Their threats and lures;
But when my eyes, alas!
  Would melt in weakness, when the charm
Of lying sin,
  Of falsest joys assures,
When a weak woman's look,
  Or fool-companions' jests, or even the calm
Bribe of ambitions hard to win
  Must make me fall,
Never to rise, wind-shook,
  And trodden down to earth,
Past a new life's recall—
  Then, Lord, I feel Thy gracious hand;
My fierce, sin-searching eyes   [birth—
  See nought but love and things of heavenly

Child-innocency, a fair band
 Of sister Charities, the zeal
Of kingly minds, the ecstasies
 Of two white souls, the beams
That speak a mother's yearnings, glances
 That simple manhood-bravery reveal.
How hast Thou blest as in fair dreams,
 Both eye and ear unmeriting,
With this Thy universe, where dances
 Flower and sunbeam, where exults
Beauty in Summer and fresh Spring ;
 Where the storm and majesty
Of Winter thunder scorn on who insults
 With folly Thy divinity !—
Oh, if Thy grace
 Has thus on me been poured,
Who share in that great death,
 And run the race
(Though feebly here)
 Of my dear Lord,
Long as I draw this breath
 Grant it me still,
And on life's prospect drear
 Let these poor eyes
Look calmly—with Heaven's light them fill,
 Pure beaming suns till death to set and rise !

GOOD FRIDAY.

WHAT is that poured-forth agony to me
Which on this day
We speak of tremblingly,
And view with silent mind,
That dares not stay,
Blinded, o'erwhelmed by what it sees,
Darkly and glancingly,
Enough the veil behind
To terrify with wonder—
Enough with fear for those who mock to freeze
Of whom am I,
Who of the day which more than Sinai's thunder
Proclaimed, think little. What
Though earth in terror oped her graves,
And fainting Death forgot
His office, giving life
To those cast up
By the earth-waves!—
All cannot overawe the strife
Of sin in this weak breast;
Nor love for who the bitter cup
Drank—the afflicted, despised,
Companionless guest,
The God without comeliness,
The King chastised,

The Bruised of the Lord,
Without guile,
Who could no less
Sweet sympathy afford—
Not only sacrifice, the smile
That speaks heart-love.
The word so dear
To grief, though never spoken
To him with pain above
All that is known to fear.
This might have broken
Sin's spell, and hushed for ever
Its uproar and tongues ;
Though while this body clothes
Its whispers never.
But with loudest lungs
To holy thought that loathes
Pride, vanity, and lust,
It speaks of each
All varyingly, ceaselessly,
Like summer flies, or dust
In clouds repeated ;
As if to make them reach
To every act,
Or that the soul may lie
Like sunshine defeated—
Lord, if it is the slave
The dull brute-body's purpose to enact,
Send still more grace.

Oh ! let not one weak soul
  Thy Son did save
Be under sin's dominion,
But give it strength to fly
Towards the heavenly goal,
  Dove-like above the wave
Of this earth, on a pinion
Death will make strong to waft beyond the sky.

EASTER-DAY.

O DEATH and Hell, what can your might
  Do now ? Ye that were lords
Of sorrow and destruction ; how are ye quite
   Subdued since He
Entered your foul dominions!—your laws and cords,
  With more than Samson-strength,
  Flung off ! This mighty conqueror, see,
   Offers to us his peace,
   To reach the length
   Of his almighty arm,
  Far as your trembling thrones, where cease
   The absolute cruelties ;
  Whose fount of lesser griefs and harm
   Is dried—earth-lusts and passions,
   The pagan joys of sense ; the lies
    Of art or intellect ;
    All fashions
    Of weak self-love ;
This life and friendship's clinging selfishness,
  The masks immortal thoughts affect—
   These fade and fail,
Death's retinue, with death retiring ;
   Since from above
  Grace came with Faith and Hope to bless
   This earthly life, and to prevail
   With heavenly shapes and voices ;
   With whispered kindnesses, desiring

Nothing to know
But pure sincerity ;
With Innocency that rejoices
In its own thoughts, and can bestow
Praise that the blush and sigh
Of Guilt repenting hope to win ;
And Honesty so clear and bold
That deeds the smallest shine,
And words of heroes seem not men—
All these can triumph o'er the spectres old :
Sickness, shame, strife,
Rome's iron fate and will,
Greece's stern camp in the domain
Of Death itself, the death-free sensual life—
All these no longer fill
The world, Hell's ensigns and the shades
Of black o'er-hovering Death.
Though tempted here and tried,
All that degrades
Can fall away; with angel-thoughts our mind
Even while we draw our breath
May glow—then what hast thou beside
Death ?   Ye Hell-minions what ?
When ev'n the body ye must find
Snatched from your grasp,
And perfected to share the soul's blest lot.
Lord give me faith that I
That out-stretched hand may clasp
Which from the grave lifts to an eternal sky.

TRINITY SUNDAY.

O MYSTERY of mysteries,
Unvisited
By our world-roving reason, whose
Wide searching eyes,
Rays from the fountain-head
Of that sun-spirit-blending
Dazzle and close ;
Though they but towards it looked,
With thought strength spending
Dark Bible-words
To picture—unrebuked,
Unshamed by weakness to behold
The rainbowed throne,
The myriad eyes and wings of birds
Around;
Then with a gaze more bold
The Father and the Sinai God,
The Friend of the Three,
The Presence shown
Where faith was found
In patriarch and prophet,—who abode
Embodied gloriously
Night-long in lightning-cloud,

G

Or blazed forth more
From 'tween the Cherubim.
Next its eyes fall
Where the Son stands, not the bowed
Gethsemane-grieving,
Not the rebuker of craft and lore
Ranked against Him
The all-wise, the all-true;
But him whom believing
Worshipped, the God-nature seen,
Now clothed with it too.
Last its eyes see
A comforting Spirit serene—
Both pity and wisdom live
In His calm face,
His hands are stretched on high
To point to heaven,
And that He thence may give
Rich gifts of grace
Unceasingly.
Then to these fainting eyes
With their last strain
'Tis given
To see but One unlikest rise
And rule alone,
Then suddenly again
To shine forth one of the Three—
Oh, wondrous!—threefold will
And action multiplied; yet one

Commingling mind !
Great One,
And Three—Justice in Love,
And holy Comfort, still
Changing to Love and Justice, find
In the depths of your wisdom and kindness
Some way from above
Into all hearts,
And give for our blindness
The gifts that each
Imparts :—
The awful reverence,
Love, and the sense
Of friendship and son-ship here.
Lonely on earth's dull beach
We shall not then sit listening,
Or sadly view the glistening
Waves of eternity, but more
Shall see and hear—
The eternal Paradise,
And its golden shore,
The hallelujahs loud
That with sweet angel-voices fall and rise,
Mixt with harp symphonies—
These be to us by you allowed,
Blest Trinity, whom this day we adore !

A PRAYER.

Lord, when the fragrant air is bright,
  And fields are shining after rain,
The glorious arch of coloured light
  Crowns with triumphant Beauty's reign.

When amid Minster pillars high
  The anthem through wide arches rings,
Then all its glories meet the eye,
  Dilating with the echoings.

When to child-beauty comes the gaze
  Of wild imaginative joy—
Not youthful spirit, genius' rays
  So clearly shine through earth's alloy.

But if thou should'st my manhood crown
  With this recipient of Thy grace,
Her tender beauty would come down
  Like dew upon a flower's face.

Her kindness and her graciousness
  Would give my life the holy peace
That weeps forth grateful humbleness,
  And glows in prayer when they increase.

O Lord, if this dear child of thine
    To my unworthiness is given,
Grant to us with the light to shine
    That beams around us from Thy Heaven.

Let worldly, unbelieving eyes
    Look on our home and see the face
Each of us turns when kind replies
    Linger to add to thought their grace.

Let them of us learn how to pray,
    And how to trust each hour Thy will,
Seeing our eyes' quick glistening ray,
    Or patient tears, with which they fill.

A PRAYER ON WHITSUNDAY.

Upon this day Thy Gracious Spirit came
And played around blest heads in tongues of flame,
It lightly flew in turn from brow to brow,
Angels as men, men did as angels show.

But since that day when Heaven-rays blessed the
    sight
Thy Spirit with eternal aureole-light
Crowns not our brows, but sits our hearts within,
And shines not through the body's cloud of sin.

None heal as with a touch, or freely speak
In tongues they from slow learning did not seek ;
The Spirit-lightnings may no longer blaze
Darkness of things of earth and sense t' amaze.

But in each heart its rule may be supreme
With truth and power on every thought to beam,
To speak the word that quenches passion's fires
And points the will to incense-pure desires ;

With truth eternal, ignorance it can bless,
And give the earthly-sorrowing, happiness—
But can Thy holy spirit sympathise,
O Lord, with what beneath such blessing lies ?

It is the Comforter, and, if to me
Such comfort in the hope of love can be,
The sunshine hope that cheers my storm-tossed mind
In that same pureness must its pure source find.

That sweet girl shines from far and seems to smile
In kindness that can all the past beguile—
Lord, as I prayed amidst that chastening gloom
I praise in faith Thy Spirit does illume.

ROGATION SUNDAY, 1879.

WEARY in heart and brain I call to Thee.
Oh, hear the sinner's call and answer me,
Thou that in heaven everlastingly
        Dwellest alone,
Father and Son, whom never eye can see,
        Bend from Thy throne !

Yearning for death and heavenly joys I find
Duties and trials fast to this earth bind,
Sin to point mocking how far, far behind
        In the heavenly race
I linger, to make duty hard and blind
        As Samson's mill-pace.

I long for love—Thou knowest how I love,
Ardour, despair, two passions through me rove :
Alas ! she cannot know, although this prove
        Madness and wrath :—
A poor heart's frenzy could not in her move
        Love to come forth.

I crave for fame, and fame is worldliness;
Yet have I thoughts that glorify distress,
That thrill delight, and people loneliness
        With Graces, Powers,
When over all this worldly pain and stress
        My glad soul towers.

I ask for Heaven, and earthly love, and fame;
Fool-hope! such self-destroying gifts to claim;
Still, I entreat Thee in Thy Son's great name,
        Almighty Lord;
I faint and fail; but Thou art still the same,
        The same Thy word.

It came to me this day; Thy house of prayer
Heard, ' Verily I say to you whate'er ' . . .
To, ' He will give it you.'—O God, I share
        With Christ Thy Son
Humanity He this day yet did wear
        Ere heavenwards gone.

DRAMATIC SKETCHES.

DRAMATIC SKETCHES.

Detached Scenes from a Dramatic Sketch

CALLED

"ISHMAEL."

DRAMATIS PERSONÆ.

ABRAHAM.	MAMRE.
ISHMAEL.	SARAH.
ELIEZER, Abraham's	HAGAR
Steward.	HAGAR'S MAID.
KING ABIMELECH.	YOUNG MEN.
ANER.	SHEPHERDS.
ESCHOL.	

ACT I. SCENE II.

AN OPEN SPACE NEAR THE TENTS.

HAGAR *meeting* ELIEZER, *the Steward.*

Eliezer.—Well, Hagar seek you shade from heat
within ?

Hagar.—Yea, and for kinder fellowship in trees,
In flowers, in the birds and beasts than Sarah.
When Abraham is forth to watch his shepherds
I must go too ; so hard to me is Sarah.

Eliezer.—Yet it were better to keep peace within.
God's peace is on my master and his house.
Disaster cannot touch him ; he's a flower
That spreads its petals boldly to the sun,
And brightens ; yet in brightest rose a canker
May poison from within ; and many a man
Domestic discord robs of peace and honour,
All but his wives accord him.

Hagar.—   Then the fault
Must be in Sarah—I stir up no discord;
Her jealousy it is ; because in me
She sees the mother of that mighty race
Which Abraham says God has promised him.
Me as a slave her malice urges her
To taunt and vex—She cannot so degrade me !
Her every word's an insolent appeal
Against God's just decision, and proves just
The curse upon her of a barren womb.

Eliezer.—Hagar, forbear this passion, which may
    tempt
The most high God to snatch from you a son
You build such boasting on. Think of that time
When with like passion you from Sarah fled :
And why you then returned.

Hagar.—I then returned, because, being faint and
    weary
A heavenly presence, as in sweetest dreams,
Spoke comfort to me ; with music blessed the ear
Dinned by my mistress' railing—and, far more,

Gave promises so liberal, I could pity
Poor chiding Sarah; with a beating heart
And with light footsteps could again return ;
Within the gloomy threshold, breathe the air,
That erst had stifled as if every other
Had been a mountain breath.

Eliezer.—   This being so,
And that for years you have borne this servitude
Why is it suddenly intolerable ?
Has the bright vision faded to your hope ?

Hagar.—No ; it grows brighter with my sweet boy's
        growth ;
My heart beats with it when I see him coming,
The fresh blood mantling his soft blooming
        cheeks,
With springing step unwearied from the field ;
Or when those lustrous eyes Egyptian suns
Gave first to me, glow, answering Abraham's
        words
And vision-weaving speech. Oh, then I see him
Beautiful as the angel of my dream.

Eliezer.—Say not thy dream ; an angel came to thee—
But if this happy promise brighter shine,
Why this impatience ?

Hagar.—   Eliezer, she my mistress
        Is tenfold harsher—can'st guess why it is so ?

Eliezer.—Yes, for I know how age must grudge the
        pleasures
It sees poured out on others.

Hagar.— 'Tis not so !
　But hoped-for joys make present pleasures tasteless.
Eliezer.—Yes ; Hagar, as she longer lives, a past
　Of longer hope deferred she must look back on.
Hagar.—I say 'tis hope she thinks ere long fulfilled,
　That wakes her long-tamed patience to revolt.
Eliezer.—Yes, Sarah hopes, and Abraham hopes too,
　That in her age she yet may have a son.
Hagar.—She thinks to have an Ishmael in the womb,
　And grieves she gave me unto Abraham.
Eliezer.—This now reminds me Abraham has said
　An angel promised it ; then lest it be,
　Submit in time ; for should this be so, Hagar,
　She will be dearer loved by Abraham,
　And you will be again a servant to her,
　Not even second though her equal now,
　By Ishmael being tied to Abraham's love,
　He will not then be sole progenitor.
Hagar.—You are as Sarah fooled by Abraham,
　Who shows as little kindness in beguiling
　Her with his dreams as he would show to me
　In now degrading me and Ishmael.
Eliezer.—Now, Hagar, what avails this jealous passion ?
　Which makes thee to blaspheme and call thy lord
　A liar and his converse with the Highest
　An idle dream.　Be wiser and submit !
　'Tis near the mid-day hour when Abraham
　Returns with all his men to shelter.　Serve
　within !—

But see where Ishmael comes, and in his hand
A man's spear, which he running balances
As if it were a staff; his eyes from his head
Look forth as though at each step he took aim,
And singled out a hundred enemies.

———

SCENE IV.

UNDER THE SHADE OF TREES IN THE HEAT
OF THE DAY.

ABRAHAM *and his* YOUNG MEN *around him.*

The flocks outspread before them.

Abraham.—Young men, exult with me in praise to God.
　　Look on this peaceful scene, these rich-fleeced
　　　flocks!
　　You that have fought with me and with me
　　　journeyed,
　　Behold the abundant fruits; contend with me
　　Once more in praise, or dumb with wonder hear
　　That richer promises are being fulfilled!
　　Then, like hushed crowds that wait to greet their
　　　prince,
　　Let acclamation swell prolonged to heaven.
　　But till these heavens have numbered the full
　　　course,

H

Till destined days have changed with light and
    darkness
Let smiles so soon to blossom into laughters
Upon all faces shine—let no one's grief
In presence of such blessings doubt that Goodness
Will quench all sorrows or bring greater blessing—
Talk out to God of them ; His ear will hear,
And though unseen, cheer more than sympathy
Of dearest friend.   But if a friend you need,
And dread to speak to such great majesty
That veils itself so oft in power and wrath,
Speak at your pressing need to God ; to me
Rehearse as to a father lesser griefs.—
Speak, Eliezer, let me with gentle breaths
Disperse the cloud that rests upon thy brow.

Eliezer.—My lord, I have no trouble, nothing dis-
    quiets me.

Abraham.—Yes, when I talked of blessings and of
    smiles
I thought you frowned.

Eliezer.—   A passing thought, no more ;
When you first spoke of wealth, my thoughts
    would swarm
Upon a little sore—the care that more wealth
    brings.

Abraham.—Thou art my faithful friend ; yet be not foe
To thine own soul, a stranger unto God—
He grant His gifts not to fix eye and mind on,
But that we more may think on Him the giver.

Think not such things can fill the mind ; they
    do so
When multiplied by avarice in thought.
Thou seest the sky is larger than the earth,
Unless with grovelling eyes we walk like beasts.
I say this but that our sons here may know
How to use wealth if it should come to them—
But speak, you two, that musing sit and whisper,
Does this care press on you, or do you scheme
To live with pleasant wealth without a care ?

1st *Young Man.*—Father, we ask not wealth nor ease,
    but honour.
This peaceful scene delights us not, although
'Tis blessing from above ; for God had given
All this and more, wrung from the heathen kings.
Think of the time when you did rescue Lot !
They tell me after that most glorious day,
The King of Sodom bowed before his greater,
The King of Salem blessed you solemnly,
But wealth you did disdain.

Abraham.—   Son, thou speak'st rashly !
'Tis fool-ambition that sets war 'bove peace ;
War is God's scourge, and when we fight we are
His feeble instruments of wrath ; we prosper
Only when humbly we obey the call.
And wilt thou make thyself the judge of sin ?
Art thou so pure ?—does sin call unto thee
Or unto heaven for vengeance ? Oh, look round ;
Tremble at swiftest judgments, more than might

Of human arm, though with God's help could
   bring.
But if thou rashly tak'st the sword, know this:
The sword unblessed can bring nor wealth nor
   peace
When both are needed most; thy life 'twill save,
But leave so many enemies that age
Will be quenched in blood, no time to thee be ⁻
   giv'n
To meditate, to speak out praise to God,
Or feel His love in promises, though dim,
That lift the wearied soul above this earth.

2nd *Young Man.*—Father, let me too speak; I do
   abjure
This self-sought honour, which must bring the
   scourge
Recoiling on a man's own head. I know
You have in calm God-fearing peace found honour
More than war most successful could have given.
Yet think if now be not the time for war,
For executing judgment, for God's wrath.
Is not God's honour slighted by Abimelech,
Who sent to take his servant's wife by force?
And when report of your exploits waked fear,
Did he not send her back with presents, gifts
Of men and women-servants—wretched salves
For God's offended honour?   Once again
I mention that great day my brother spoke of:
Was it not for avenging Lot's indignity,

And far more—their contempt of God who
    wrought it,
That then with solemn ceremony kings
Went forth to meet the conqueror returning
And on him showered such blessing that heaped
    spoil
Seemed dross and worthless chaff?

Abraham.—   And who, my son,
Who can suppose himself God's champion?
Who can lean always on His promises?
Who, free from passion, with obedient heart
Can listen for God's voice, then against sin
No inward frailty welcomes, take the sword,
And with eye fixed wait the great Captain's word?
Beware, lest thou attribute to thy God
Thy earth-born passions, thy vain-glory name
His honour, or 'midst uproar of ambitions,
Of strifes in thine own breast, hear them com-
    manding.
Know too, that war is but one punishment.
If chosen by the Highest, perform it humbly.
Thou talk'st of my exploits; but mine eyes flashed
Nor my cheeks flushed in highest victory
As thine have done in but recalling them.
His terror dwelt with me but little less
Than with mine enemies—this insult given
How know'st thou 'tis not on Abimelech
Avenged already? How if God,
Not by an arm of flesh, but by His voice

His presence has this trembling soul affrighted,
Or sent some secret scourge upon his household !—
Forbear then ! cease this boastful warrior strain ;
'Tis impious : ráther fear lest thou offend
By thy presumption more than the offenders
Thou deem'st so ripe for punishment.

Eliezer.—   My lord !
Two shepherds here desire to speak to you.

Abraham.—Bid them stand forth ; they are men of
    peace.   How oft,
Returning from some hill-side, where celestials
Had been my company, has their plain speech
And simple thinking, 'kin to the dignity
Of nature's thousand forms and sounds, not
    jarred
Upon my mind uplifted but recalled
With gentle summons ; like the golden light
That wakens from sweet dreams—But, Eliezer,
I like not that !

Eliezer.—What like you not, my lord ?

Abraham.—What means that spear in the young
    shepherd's hand ?
I have not seen such since the day I armed
All of my household.   Now is mine anger stirred,
If you my sons, that spoke in praise of war,
Have armed anticipating my command,
Ev'n now perhaps strife begun—yes, there is
    blood.
Speak, man, who's is it on that spear ?

Young Shepherd.— My lord,
I found this by your tent.

1st Young Man.— And we, my lord,
Know nothing of the matter; think not we,
Though youth's blood prompt us would usurp
command;
Call not our zeal rebellion.

Abraham.— Say then, shepherd,
What mean you by thus bringing to my presence
This bloody spear?

Young S.— My lord, I found it by your tent.
My father here says this is blood of sheep,
And as he thinks, some thief has here been busy,
Then thrown the spear, to 'scape suspicion, from
him.
Because I would not have you robbed though
mine,
I say my flock tended with care these five years,
I have not lost one from; this blood's of sheep
From other shepherd's fold—then now I offer
My service to you to find whence 'tis missing,
And who has taken it.

Eliezer (aside).— This is the spear
Young Ishmael carried, that he flung aside
On entering Hagar's tent. How easily
I might explain and get this clown dismissed;
But tongue be dumb, for if it must be told
I'll not exalt the boy more, so to make
My own climb harder.

Old Shepherd.—My son has said what's true.
We found the spear all bloody where he said ;
And from the fold, my lord, I've lost a sheep
Which I supposed had strayed—what need of
    more ?
I will no further speak ! the times are peaceful ;
And, nothing heard, this must be blood of sheep
That silent died, first driven to some tent.
Abraham.—If this be so, have you, has any one
Suspicion of the thief or slenderest clue
By which to find him ?
Young S.—   My lord, this man,
My father, who has served you long, and I,
Who will as long serve with like faithfulness,
Till I am old as he is—we both think
You do yourself some wrong in trusting much
These servants given by King Abimelech.
Old S.—Son, by your leave—My lord, I did but say,
That, being town-bred, unused to large flocks,
They were unapt at service and did need
Directions so repeated that our labours
Seemed ever growing.
Young S.—   Nay, father, bear me out.
You thought, and I too thought, both weighing
    more
Our master's profit than our own, if guilt
Should fall on any for a deed like this
It must be on those who so lately served
The strong thief King Abimelech.

Old S.— My lord,
One of these men I certainly did hear
In converse with thy oldest servant say,
That God could not have been with you in battle
Upon that day you rescued Lot, because
That wicked King of Sodom joined with you.
Abraham.—But you, who fought with me, what did
　you say?
Did you not bear God witness?
Old S.— Aye, my lord.
But silently, your other servant spoke
Against this villain, I stopped my ears and ran
To lose his blasphemy, and be assured
He is like to have committed this less crime.
Abraham.—And how much better 'twould thine age
　have fitted
To have enlightened this poor ignorant man!
How ill this rancour suits with thy grey hairs,
A crown of glory if they shade a face
With goodness and with wisdom eloquent!
But this unkind, ill-founded jealousy
Demands some punishment.—Bind these men
　both of them,
That on this slight ill-woven tale hang slanders
And baseless calumnies.—Thou prating knave,
　　　　　　　　　　　　[*To* Young S.]
Art thou so simple, or does passion blind thee,
To think men would kill sheep with spears?
　That blood

May be a man's and shed by thee in quarrel;
The words repeated here that there were mixed
With murderous blows—Take both of them away,
And feed on bread and water. [SHEPHERDS *led out.*
    I'll inquire
If any of my servants now are missing,
If any have received a wrong—Young men
If any wish my favour, come not thus
With loud complaint of fancied wrongs or real;
If fancied, yet proclaimed with confidence,
How must red shame defend itself with lies,
And the offended ne'er be reconciled!
Such flaming wrath and such a wall of shame
Will spring 'tween reconciliation! But,
If real let th' offended one think this,
That he too may have erred, that the offence
Was perhaps repented of, and the offender
Ready to mingle tears, which shame now dries
And turns to sparkling wrath, the downcast lids
Veiling defiance. Follow not these men!
Admit not basest jealousy; your fellows
Rather treat kindly. We dwell in the light,
Recipients of gracious promises!
All kings, if peace of mind and bodies' safety
No less ennoble than rich robes and pomp,
With retinues. Let then these starved souls grow,
These darkened minds have light! But where to-
    day
Is my beloved son Ishmael? he should have heard

With brightening face my teachings ; yet, to say
   truth,
Glad am I for his innocent boyhood he
Has not been witness of this saddening malice ;
And our first speeches made in praise of war
He happily escaped.   I grieve, beholding
His blood with such themes easily takes fire—
Where is he ?

Eliezer.—My lord, I saw him near the mid-day hour
   At Hagar's tent.

Abraham.—   Then, young men, to your duties
   Till setting of the sun.   I'll presently
   Go in to find my son.   Come, Eliezer.

                        [*Exeunt.*

END OF ACT I.

ACT II.   SCENE I.

ISHMAEL *asleep*—HAGAR *by him.*

Hagar.—Sleep on my precious boy! From thy smooth
  brow
I lift this straying curl, and place it where
It floats with the black ripples on the pillow.
What a holy calm broods o'er the smooth full
  eyelids !
Which glow with light like clouds that veil the
  sun.
See, from the silver veils dark fringes sweep
To touch his cheek ! What sweet unconsciousness
Is in those lips, parted with pretty pout !
How gently heaves with each life-giving breath
That smooth white front. These rounded limbs
Now careless flung are oh, how full awake
Of spring and suppleness !—their morning freedom
Has made them early prisoners, on them lies
A death-like stillness ; quiet sleep embraces,
Turning to sculptured grace their cunning beauty.

SCENE III.

SARAH'S TENT.

SARAH—HAGAR'S MAID.

Sarah.—Well, I will do my best and intercede
To spare thy lover's life. Now dry your eyes!
So you poor innocent would be a mother!
God grant your wish, and make you happier
Than I your mistress!
Maid.— God bless you, madam,
Would I could make you happier.
Sarah.— Something thou canst do.
Maid.—All I can do is heartily at your service.
Sarah.—Then pray to God for me! He hears the
    prayer
Of innocent virgins such as you are. You
Have never felt temptation's fiercest, know not
A past without a hope ; with you experience
Brings joys unlooked for; all is pleasure with you;
And what's to come still brighter. You did
    never
Gaze on a sunlike hope until the eye
Of your poor mind was closed to every other;
Or with rash malice quench the light of faith
And cherish sullenly your grief amidst
The darkness of ingratitude.
Maid.— Oh, madam,
Would I were good as you are : I can promise

I'll weep for you, but sure I am my prayers
Would naught avail if yours remain unanswered.
Sarah.—Well, girl, weep not for me ; thou dost
    rebuke me.
I pray God quickly may fulfil His promise,
That I may laugh, my tears be tears of joy.
(*Aside.*) Remember, God, my tears, forget that laugh
    That preluded these tears and mocked Thy
    promise.
(*Aloud.*) Now, girl, forgive my self-abandonment ;
Thou hast thy present sorrow, which to thee
Is great who could'st not bear the weight of
    mine.
I will thy master Abraham solicit
In a convenient mood. Yet tell me now,
Why didst thou not ask Hagar for this favour,
Who is thy oftener mistress ?
Maid.—   Madam, I did.
I asked her. Most unkindly she refused me.
Sarah.—   She wisely doubted p'rhaps her influence
With Abraham.
Maid.—   That was her poor excuse,
So faintly spoken that a child might see
She knew herself to be possessed of it ;
But of the precious ware would not one scruple
Consent to barter for my poor advantage.
Sarah.—That was her sole excuse ? she would
    vouchsafe
No other to you ?

Maid.—   Oh yes ;—that these new servants
From King Abimelech were honest people,
And ought not to be blamed maliciously.
Sarah.—And did she praise the honourable king ?
Or blame him that he rather had not chosen
Her for his chance-come wife ?
Maid.—   She said not so ;
But that he would have done us all a kindness,
Had he still kept possession of yourself.
Sarah.—She dared not say so !—this shall Abraham—
Well, girl, he shall soon know of your request.
Now leave me ; he will soon return, and I
Must first prepare myself against his coming.

[*Exit* MAID, *and* SARAH *to inner part of tent.*

SCENE IV.

AN OPEN SPACE.

ABRAHAM—HAGAR—ISHMAEL.

Hagar.—My lord, I pray thee has Eliezer told you
Aught to the advantage of dear Ishmael,
Anything in his praise ?
Abraham.—   I think no, Hagar.
Thou hast such appetite to hear his praises,

That I could never keep them from thee, should
What man soever speak them.   I will now
Myself a little praise him.   See, what fine poise,
With what a grace he balances himself,
To watch what there has stirred within that bush,
What bird or beast—all creatures known to him !
Not their eyes are so keen (not half so beautiful)
Nor their soft feet so silent in their footing
As are his footsteps, moving unconsciously,
Elastic with the spring of boyhood, timed
To boyhood's spirits.

Hagar.—Well, you have praised the son so much, the
    mother
So left out from the praise grows jealous, fearing
At first you would come short, as you proceed,
She calms at hearing justice dealt upon
Her dearest in full measure ; but in the end
Finds what she deemed impossible, herself
Grudging her son his treasure, thirsting for
One drop from his o'erflowing fountains.

Abraham.—   Yes ;
The treasure of such health, such spirits, sleep
That comes uncalled, folding the body round
As soft and closely as a mother's arms,
And giving it to life fresh as a dew-washed
    flower.
We all feel envious of such sweet gifts
That once have been our own, and which for ever
We would have ours.   But why so sad, Hagar ;

This though so grave is yet a common loss
As each puts on the man or woman.

Hagar.—   Yes ;
And is there no sweet gift, no power, no
    passion
For man and woman, which, alas, that 'tis not!
Is too oft none of theirs ?   Is there no life,
No sweet refreshing, tender languishment,
No fire that kindles at the heart, that throbs
Through pulse and brain, that looks out at the eyes
All in a moment ?   This is life indeed,
Beyond weak childhood's.   They will find it so
Who carry the poor ashes of a heart,
And look from beamless sockets on the past,
With the eyes of the grave.

Abraham.—   Why, what means this ?
Why suddenly dost thou breathe out these curses ?
Against whom ?

Hagar.—   Myself, my lord !

Abraham.—   Thyself !   Why so ?
Why dost thou curse thyself in health and beauty?
Thy eyes are beaming through thy tears, then
    why
Condemn them to the grave ?

Hagar.—   Ah, my lord, listen !
And ere the look of scorn fly to thy face,
Before the word of cold contempt fall crushing
On my poor heart, ere as from viper-jaws
The poison flash forth on me—hear me but speak!

I

Abraham.—Say on; I change not countenance, nor
    speak
    One word till thou hast eased thy heart. Most
      gladly
    Would I by listening banish thy sad looks
    For ever, Hagar.

Hagar.—   Ah, how sweet is pity
    Coming from thee! then hear me, dearest lord.
    I long have watched thee, but to learn what
      pleased,
    Or what brought shadows to thy face; what fired
    Thine angry eye; what speech would droop thy
      lids,
    Or circle them with large o'erpowering thoughts.
    If any news, whate'er may happen, I
    Can tell what look 'twould bring thee; at a
      glance
    I read in thy face all that happens to thee.
    I have a maid who calls this magic; know,
    'Tis love, who quickly learns, whose memory
    Is ever young.—But more, I'll tell thee more!
    This care each hour to learn, to please, to answer,
    With cheerful brave humility for years
    All unrewarded soared at the highest pitch,
    Still singing with new force its heavenly notes
    Far o'er a clamorous self-deafening world;
    Its strength fed by a heart whose fulness could
    No measure find for its large gifts of love.
    But now, alas! it 'gins to flag, to falter.

Must then, my lord, this faithful servant perish?
Need it grow aged or toil worn? Speak one word
To make it young again; one moment now
Of love like to its own, to answer to its years,
Would be a draught of youth perennial.
Abraham(aside).—How easy 'twere, how hard
          'tis to forbear
To look into those melting eyes, to clasp
In passionate embrace that yielding form,
Then find ourselves together in the midst
Of a new world, where all is brightness, all
Uncloying everlasting happiness.
(*Aloud.*) 'But know this, Hagar, such a moment's
          bought
With all this life's collected happiness,
Its light all gathered to this falling star;
This fierce extreme, if answered by another,
Must fall by its own weakness; but, unanswered,
Turns to as fierce extreme of hate; both soon
Are neither love nor hate; our mortal grossness
Forbids our spirit the strong love of angels
Or hate of devils. Give best love to God,
And make no man thine idol. He can give
Richest return, and temper so thy love
With awful reverence that it shall be
No fierce extreme akin to tiger hate.
Ev'n so love me—say not thou'rt in my power,
I love thee; but thou'rt free to love God more.
Nor think that I can give thee that great love

Which I long since have given to my God.
Oh, cease to ask it ! think no more of it ;
We may not here beneath God's eye adventure
One moment's rapture for a life's true peace
And peaceful truth.   [*Exit.*
Hagar.—   And peaceful falsehood !
Death of the soul, stagnation and corruption !
Apostasy from that great god of truth
In each true breast !   O, thou great god of love,
Forgive that I have spent thy precious gifts
Upon a soulless wretch that scorned them all.
Make me the channel now of bitter curses
Great as thy blessings ; give me cunning now
To be a serpent's, let me embracing kiss
And poison as I kiss ; let kindness dwell
Still in my face, a traitor to give up
All bravery to hideous massacre,
All innocence to lust and butchery.
I will devise most hideous slanders, rest
I'll scare with whispered treacheries, all proved
Against his dearest ; his bed shall now be thorns,
His honour blackened so (while pent-up shame
Shall see no proof to let its vengeance forth),
Himself as pierced and helpless as
In some wild dream !   The saintly Sarah too,
I will her whiteness mire with calumny.
Hark, this way comes the steward Eliezer,
A slavish parasite ; yet might I win
His interest in my conspiracies.

Enter ELIEZER.

Eliezer.—Not yet within? Who's stirring here with
thieves,
Adulterers and base conspirators?

Hagar.—'Tis I; but why from you, Eliezer, comes
This passionate impatience?

Eliezer.—Ah, Hagar! Is it you? Forgive that once
I chode you, using fierce and angry words
Against our master Abraham. The like
Are ready now at my lips, and but a sigh
Wafts them to yours again.

Hagar.— Then give them me.
The love I bear my lord will lighten them;
Yet all the weight you feel I too will feel
With kindest sympathy.

Eliezer.— Then listen, Hagar.
As I now parted from him just returned,
Ere we changed greeting, 'God watch over you,'
I whispered to him, 'Think again, my lord;
My son deserves that post.' To which he
answers,
His countenance as black as wind-heaped clouds
That thunder bursts, 'And did thy subtle wife
Teach thee her wicked importunity?'
Then, seeing anger pale me he proceeds,
'Forgive me; what was I saying here, Eliezer?'
I would have answered him, but he again
Bursts in with, 'Trouble me no more, and leave
me.'

Hagar.—Well, he was chafed; something had troubled
  him.
Eliezer.—And is it then on me, his faithful steward,
  His counsellor, his right hand—is it on me
  He vents his anger ?   Should he hide from me
  His own grief, and, much worse, give me a bitt'rer ?
Hagar.—No ; but you speak of one whose heart is
  marble.
  Your wisest counsel he would deem not yours
  But God's that speaks through you to him ; you
  are
  No more but His mere instrument that served ;
  And not a friend to whom sweet gratitude
  Is due.   He would not stick to cast you off,
  Be sure.
Eliezer.—If I thought so, then be assured
  I would pay him nor gratitude nor service ;
  I would deserve his base ingratitude.
  If I must be called thief, being honest, I
  Will handle wealth untoiled for ; if in youth
  I had been falsely censured for my wildness,
  I would have swum in seas of lust ; much wine
  Should have consumed, and quarrel ended me.
  But tell me Hagar, why comes this from you,
  What prompts you now to speak such words of
  him ;
  To talk of his ' marble heart ' ?
Hagar.—   First spoken now,
  But whispered by my heart these many years—

If you perceive but base ingratitude,
What freezings, harsh repulses, what forced cheer,
And frowning 'gainst her smiles his wife has
    known ;
Yea, and the wife who's borne a son to him.
When each might claim, the one for the other's
    sake
One look of love their way, one wide embrace
To clasp them to his heart together—look you !
He but commends us to his God and leaves us.
Eliezer (aside).—This Hagar meditates some wicked-
    ness ;
She speaks thus fiercely or to draw me on
Or else to sound my mind and win me to her.
I'll seem to yield that I may know her secret.
(*Aloud.*) Then, Hagar, suffer it no longer ; show him
The power you have to pain as well as please.
You know how I am galled ; that there is nothing
You can devise against him I'll not second—
I who am aged with thought both night and day
To plan success and build prosperity,
Yet knew it must pace quicker as this grew
And sow a wrinkle at each step—the heart
And faculties all dulled that might enjoy
What his successes shared me—I must now
Not only have endured these toils and losses,
But see the prize snatched from my wearied
    hands—
My o'er-toiled self driven out.

Hagar.—   I'm glad of this !
Now we'll together work to punish him—
Not for revenge, thou would'st not have revenge ?
Eliezer.—Yes, for revenge ; I thirst for it.
Hagar.—   Thou dost not !
Thou play'st me false.   For what can he have
    done
To call revenge from thee ?
Eliezer.—   I say for thee !
My wrong demands but punishment, but thine
Calls loudly for revenge.
Hagar.—   Then now, attend !
We'll strike at him through Sarah ; she's the one
That he best loves ; then what if we could win
Abimelech once more to rob us of her
And this time not to yield her back !
Eliezer.—   How keenly
This would vex Abraham—'twere thy revenge.
Hagar.—Not so !   I said that she was his best-loved ;
    But with no heart to love, if she were dead
    He would but mourn for her a fortnight's space.
    We can but hope to taint and wound his honour ;
    This will be punishment but no revenge.
Eliezer.—Then am I glad ; I would not have revenge.
Hagar.—Thy part would be upon the appointed day
    To give his servants opportunity,
    To see our young men with the servants busied
    In distant labours, then to check pursuit.
    I have a maid of subtle tongue, and she

Shall with her lover to Abimelech.
She can persuade him Sarah longs for him,
Extol her grace, and tell of her languishment,
That the exploit is easy, and is much
Expected of him.
Eliezer.—　　　　　　　　　I will do my part.
But who is your maid's lover?
Hagar.—　　　　　　　　　That same shepherd
Who brought to Abraham the bloody spear,
And now is kept a prisoner with his father.
Eliezer.—Then he must first be freed; we need but
　say
The spear was Ishmael's; had I been there　　　'
I had myself explained and spared him this;
I'll tell our master Abraham.
Hagar.—　　　　　　　　　　But you—
Were you not present when they brought the
　spear?
They told me you brought them.
Eliezer.—　　　　　　　　　They told you true.
But I was called away and heard no more;
I could not then remember that the spear
Was what young Ishmael carried.
Hagar.—　　　　　　　　　　Forget again;
Let Abraham still think it the shepherd's.
Eliezer.—Then, how can he go to Abimelech?
Hagar.—Let some suspicion still be clinging to him;
Then will these injured servants help our plot.
He can be freed and sent, it shall be said,

A little while in exile, which will be
Our wanted opportunity to send him.

Eliezer.—The spear shall not be Ishmael's, nor the
blood
The blood of wolf—how well all hangs together !
Let us now part and speak again to-morrow.

[*Exeunt.*

END OF ACT II.

ACT III.   SCENE I.

TIME, EARLY MORNING—A GRASSY VALLEY.

*Young Men exercising on horseback and foot with
blunted spears and swords.*

1st *Young Man.*—Have at you again ! I was killed
by you
And now rise up to be a fresh assailant,
Although half spent. I hope when 't comes to
fighting,
My adversary will be something weaker,
Or I more skilful.
2nd *Young Man.*—   Brother, I shall be,
When the day comes for fighting on, your side.
We have so fortified our weaknesses
That none shall stand against us.
1st *Young Man.*—   You have learnt
My weaknesses, and where I am too rash ;
But I know not where you're assailable ;
You have both strength and cunning, I but
strength.
2nd *Young Man.*—Upon the day of battle all are
strangers ;

And each stands up with strength, nor fear we
cunning,
But help each one the other.

Another part of the meadow.

1*st Young Man.*—Well, while we breathe our horses
tell me now
To what end is all this?
2*nd Young Man.*—　　　All what? this exercise?
1*st Young Man.*—What is its purpose?
2*nd Young Man.*—Thou should'st have asked this
Ere my arm wearied ; I could have cuffed thee,
then,
To excellent purpose.
1*st Young Man.*—I understand thee then to say,
This exercise can make the fist reply
Where the tongue fails ; is this wit used as well
Against a friend as enemy?
2*nd Young Man.*—　　　Against a friend
Who makes his tongue no better that a fist,
And idly beats the air, against the enemy
Not to be idly beating air oneself.
1*st Young Man.*—Then, marry, friend! so wilt thou
then not need
To come to exercise ; for women's tongues
Are fists that beat the husband's ears, and thou
Might'st then cuff on for using tongues as fists
That idly beat the air.

2nd Young Man.—Women ! who talks of women ?
I tremble for you, brother ; I never knew
A resolute, valiant man who talked of them :
They've wit—not wisdom; beauty but not strength.
I'll fight for women, but not stay with them.

1st Young Man.—Thou art a fool ! When I first
asked my question,
It was but to lead on to this plain answer ;
There is no life but pleasure, no reward,
If toil makes not enjoyment sweeter.

2nd Young Man.— Well,
Thou wilt be pleasure's slave, as much outworn
And wearied in its service as the furrowed
And horny-fisted toilers. I must hope
That thorny labour will hedge in and spur thee
Betimes from thy down bed, giving thy life
Some sweetness.

1st Young Man.— For thee, I hope some dame
Will cross thine eye, and soften in her lap
From very shame thy fierce disdains ; will take
From thy revenges some fool-hardiness,
And make thee once or twice before thou diest
Forgive a wronger.

2nd Young Man.—Well, be not moved ; we both
May still be proud of wit and strength ; if these,
When we shall meet hereafter shall be found
The one or other lacking, 'twill be women.

1st Young Man.—And if—let these words bring us
truce—the devils

Ambition, pride, self-boastfulness, contempt,
Be exorcised and banished, 'twill be women.

Another part of the meadow.

1*st Young Man.*—We are exercised and valiant! give
    us war!
Let our lord Abraham lead us forth, or leave us
Ourselves to seek out exploits and adventures!
2*nd Young Man.*—He lead us forth! we might be
    cowards; shames,
Indignities he'll let be heaped upon him.
'Tis coming age that dulls his judgment, and
Abates his vigour. He does think we all
Are past exploits as he is.

Enter ISHMAEL.

1*st Young Man.*—Ishmael, when you are master, will
    you not
Lead forth our strength, and under your captain-
    ship
Shall we not all, with eager step and eye,
Seek out new dangers, and be crowned with
    glory?
Ishmael.—I'll prove myself your captain by the share
I take of hazard; who takes more, and wins
More glory, him I'll serve as captain. We shall
    all
Compete as cheerful as reward; no action
Shall unrewarded die.

1st Young Man.— That's to be stirring !
Curse on these sleepy times ! A day will be
More precious then than a year is now. We shall
Much grudge these misspent years.

2nd Young Man.— Thou'lt not endure
To let a villain king, a heathen lecher,
Send out his army to fetch in your wife,
To add to his wife-army !

Ishmael.— Of whom do you talk ?

2nd Young Man.—Of Abraham, thy father; I say
thou—

Ishmael.—I will not hear a word in his dispraise;
If you must praise me but by robbing him
Of his true praise, speak not another word :
I will not act perhaps like him, when as he
I am a man ; but if a man of any pith
My bravery will be but what his was.

Both.— Heaven keep you !
We'll serve you too as faithfully, be sure,
And far more willingly, than we serve him.

Another part of the meadow.

Enter ABRAHAM *and* OLD SERVANT.

Abraham.—The God of heaven bless you, my brave
sons !
You bring back noblest youth to me. I see
In your fixed serious eyes and manly gestures,
Your grace and quickness—in all these I see

Beauty unsullied, sweet grave dignity,
A spirit wrought up thirsting for great deeds,
Done for themselves in scorn of flattery,
Or bribes of wealth and pleasure. If purity
Thus shine from within while strength rides on
　　your arm,
Doubt not God's favour; your mind's fortitude
Will then, be certain, guide your actions with
A royal judgment; it shall never need
To stoop for flattery, or soothing, or delight
(That softens not relieves) in the arms of women.—
Are all our servants here, the new ones mustered?
Young Man.—I know not; shall I look to it, my lord?
Abraham.—Go, I would have all virtuous and brave,
　　　　　　　　　　　　[*Exit* YOUNG MAN.
Though courage be with virtue gone awhile,
From ill examples town life brought them.—Say
　　thou,
Did thy wife tempt thee? hast thou thus faithful
　　been,
Through much domestic discord?
Old Servant.—　　　　　　　　No; my lord,
May God be with her soul—she was obedient, as
In service to you, faithful.
Abraham.—　　　　　　　There be some such,
That shine with light reflected: thy sun-goodness
Made her beam faintly; there's an awe in some
Towards nobler natures; she saw angrily
Thou could'st not be seduced.

Old Servant.— My lord, I pray you,
Speak not in your high wisdom such dread censure,
Or I must think it proved; yet not once
I saw her angry with this base intent,
To drive me to ingratitude.

Abraham.— I speak not
Knowing of aught against her, but if thus
As true and simple as thou speakest her,
I say thou hast been blessed above the wise,
The rich, the noble. From ten thousand women
Thou hast picked one, the chiefest—all the rest
Weigh not together that one.

Old Servant.— Well, my lord,
I would believe you for a greater wonder;
This passes my dull understanding; but
My mind so long has leant upon you, I
Must still believe your oracle; should error
Come now to you, yourself must tell me so.
The opposite I'll but from you believe.
You've shown me how your goodness is re-
warded;
I've learned from you how to find God in life,
Not in the clouds and skies.

Abraham.— But think'st thou not
He is a spirit that walks earth and skies?

Old Servant.—My lord, I see He blesses you; I know
not.
I have been blessed when I have walked as you.
[*Re-enter* YOUNG MAN.

Young Man.—My lord, of these new servants one cannot be found.

He is missing; no trace of him for this two days.

Abraham.—Why, where is he? not with the flocks;
He is

No shepherd—them have I seen this morning,

                      [Enter ELIEZER.

Eliezer, know you why there's missing now
One of our servants given by Abimelech?

Eliezer.—My lord, I know not, nor did know him
missing.

Abraham.—See that his place is filled, and meanwhile
search.

Eliezer.—My lord, if you should want the fullest
numbers,

Those two are prisoners who brought the spear;
They might be freed, since nothing's brought
against them.   [to me

Abraham.—The father and the son, who brought
The bloody spear and railed upon their fellows?

Eliezer.—The same! they have been punished for
their railing;

The younger would be married.

Abraham.—   That shows him foolish,
And soon to prove most wicked; being a fool,
His wife will sway his actions and bring forth
Her hoarded wickedness.

Eliezer.—   My lord, you are harsh in this;
They may be fools together.

Abraham.— In God's eyes, doubtless.
But in man's eyes, he's the simpler—talk not of
    him.
Let him be left ; he's harmless where he is.
Inquire more strictly, has he not learnt quarrel
From one speech with this woman—that man
    missing—
Has he left complaint? Have the old man released !

          [*Exit* ABRAHAM *and* OLD SERVANT.

SCENE IV.

ABRAHAM *and* SARAH *in a tent—*SARAH *lying on
a bed—*ABRAHAM *sitting by her.*

Sarah.—Thanks to the God of Heaven—my God and
    my Lord !
Oh, I can scarcely speak, my heart so swells
With gratitude ; scarcely can I look up—
So well my eyes with tears of thankfulness;
The heavy burden that I've borne these years
Is eased ; a balm has soothed, a comfort cheered.
The aching sad reproach that ever sat
Beyond sweet patience' cure at my poor heart.
God, thou hast eased my heart when it was
    breaking,

And with a joy far greater than the sorrow
Hast made it laugh again with hope fulfilled!

Abraham.—O dear-loved wife, how art thou blessed;
what woman
Has had the birth of such a longed-for child
So gloriously heralded ? Those three shining
ones,
Who honoured so this earth—that they should
deign
To grace this dwelling with their presences!
And speak such gracious words, accompanied
With gestures of such awful dignity!

Sarah.—Yet leave not out, to humble me and teach me
To be more grateful—how I did mock in my
heart
With scornful laughter such as one might use
To humblest mortals !

Abraham.—   Forget it, dearest wife,
As it had never been ; thou see'st that God
Has given the freest pardon with this blessing
That thy laugh doubted—thou didst believe
Them mortals:—the woman spending thought
and care
With cheerful humbleness on lower duties
Oft finds her wings too weak to soar above them.
Thy poor heart yearned so, that the sudden promise
Seemed to mock it !

Guard (without).—   My lord Abraham !

Abraham.—Who calls? come in and speak your message.

Enter GUARD.

Guard.—Master, I come in duty bound to tell you
The prisoners have been released as you
Did send us word; we wait dismissal.

Abraham.—The old man I gave freedom to—the younger
It is your duty still to guard.

Guard.—My lord, they are both released—the first
By your word through your steward Eliezer,
The younger by your word that came through Hagar,
Who sent her maid with escort to conduct him
Into short exile, there to wait until
His strife-provoking speeches are forgotten.
This was the message brought that you had sent.

Abraham.—Then Hagar sent it and not I—Enough !
Let all be free and joyous on this day.
He shall have freedom ; and your slackness too
Comes on a day on which 'tis discipline ;
Go spread the news and let all faces beam
And hands be raised to God in thankfulness
For sending me this day a son.

[*Exit* GUARD.

Sarah.—Was it the shepherd who had brought to you
A bloody spear round which he wove suspicions ?

Abraham.—It was ; he taught me with ill-judged suspicions
To be of him suspicious with rash judgment.

Sarah.—Then he it was that Hagar's maid entreated
    With tears and strong petition I should urge you
    Freely to pardon and restore to favour.
Abraham.—And now it seems she has won her mistress
    Hagar
    To furnish her with escort for his rescue.
    Well, she is cunning and may marry him !
    I hope he may not find beneath her rule
    A bondage heavier than ours, a punishment
    More grievous, though his tongue be now o'er-
    crowed
    And innocent of slander.
    (*Aside.*)   Her mistress taught it her.
    The soft and tender heart of that kind woman
    Could not let them languish ; her heart took fire ;
    She is a champion in Love's cause—the haste !
    To send an escort with the maid to head it,
    And give discharge at once if he were bound—
    No time to ask my leave ! Thy passion is
    Fierce as a tigress, as supple and as certain as
    Its spring !—how tame to this seems thought and
    wisdom,
    Approved and gentle feeling, all response
    Of meditation or sure intuition ;
    To this wrought passion, thundering on its course
    Towards high'st success or irretrievable destruction.
Sarah.—Why is my lord so moody ? why that staring
    With earnest looks on vacancy ? you were now
    All sunshine ; bidding others smile you frown.

Abraham.—Dear wife, calm noble-hearted woman,
These sun-like joys must be right humbly borne;
Gazed on too eagerly they blind and sadden ;
Feeding my heart too full with them, it beckoned
A fasting sorrow—the sense of recent frailty,
And too much yielded to temptation.
Sarah.—Then, as thou badest me some short time since
Safely dismiss in presence of such blessings
All thought of weaknesses that threatened them ;—
So I entreat you now, mar not the peace,
The dignity of the uplifted heart, with thoughts
That tempest it with worldly strifes and passions.
Abraham.—Sweet woman! the peace of heaven is upon
    thee.
Thou pourest from thy love-o'erflowing heart
The sweet and liberal graces of young children.
And with my spirit I have drunk of them
At its refreshing fountain. I go forth
To keep it clear, unsoiled, unvisited
By venomous creatures or the falling leaves
That passion's winds have blasted. Sleep thou
    here,
Shrouded by angels' wings !—She is asleeep !
Smiling in peace as innocent as her child ;
The invisible angels whisper to her in dreams,
And with their rustling wings, unheard awake,
Tune soft sphere-music to her wondering ear.
                [*Exit* ABRAHAM.

SCENE VI.

ABRAHAM *and* ELIEZER *in a tent—*SARAH *asleep.*

Abraham.—What man, why look so pale, why dost
  thou tremble,
When I do tell thee that I know of it?
I knew he had escaped; I knew who sent him;
'Twas done in a rebellious spirit doubtless,
A head-strong passion ever rules that woman,
And draws all to it—'tis a fascination,
I know its cause and what has led to it—
Yea, and must soon, too soon, bewail its course.
Thou art pale at this, the end foreshadowing.
Be brave, methinks that I can see yet farther,
Yet sympathise with her as much as thou.
Eliezer.—O my lord, pardon me. I confess all to thee—
Yea, all that ever passed 'twixt her and me
Shall now come forth, and you shall judge of it;
I with much sorrow and entreaty for forgiveness,
Now tell thee—
Abraham.—Tell me nothing, ask not to be forgiven.
Thou need'st it not, I know thee, Eliezer,
How faithfully, with what unwearied patience
Thou hast preserved in peace my growing wealth,
Commanded all my household, ta'en the care,
And left the comfort of prosperity—

Tax me not now to utter forth thy praises—
They're known to all, and I do feel them most ;
But what could vigilance prevail to check
Imperious passion, that like a raging sea
Cannot be stopped, but must be yielded to,
And left to dash in vain against the rock
Of calm, well-ordered reason :—'tis a nature
All in arms ; a populace armed.   If thou
Would'st muster every faculty for one,
One mighty rush as of an avalanche,
Thou mightest then oppose it ; but thou know'st
That this is reason's, feeling's suicide
To give mad passion ten-fold life.

Eliezer (aside).—He knows not then my share in it—
        I am safe.   [say'st,

(*Aloud.*) My lord, thou speak'st of Hagar—as thou
    My vigilance could never check her passion.
    But must it not forewarn you—would you be
    Its victim unprepared?

Abraham.—No, Eliezer, I would be prepared ;
    I would save her from the bitter penalty
    This passion pays.

Eliezer.—   You know what she intends
    By sending this young shepherd with his wife
    To King Abimelech ?

Abraham.—   To keep him from the sight
    Of angry eyes his falsehood kindled here.

Eliezer.—My lord, ask me not how I have discovered ;
    But 'tis to move Abimelech to come

With force to fetch away your wife there sleeping,
Who this day bore you that most precious son.
Abraham.—It cannot be—she would not venture this !
Has she so little knowledge ?   How know'st this ?
Eliezer.—Ask me not how !—I know it—Hagar's anger,
Her haste in freeing him, the maid she sent,
She has a subtle tongue my lord—all these
Prove that this is so.
Abraham.—   All these are but surmises ?
Good Eliezer, here thy zeal's suspicion,
A fault of age and one I must forgive,
But thou know'st not this Hagar as I know her—
She is most proud, most passionate—her heart
Is given or lost, and ever noble she,
Of a spirit, always in extremes, will aye
Command, or else bewail with tenderness,
That never looks up but to frown on fate :
It is not wretched malice 'gainst all others.
Now come with me ; I fear lest louder talk
Awaken Sarah ;—I have much to give thee
Of necessary counsel.   We must celebrate
This joyful day with feasting.   I would all
With me should joy ; while pleasant tasteful food
Cheers and invigorates, I would all smiled,
And seated round me answered my glad looks,
With eyes that beam reflecting gratitude.
                                        [*Exeunt.*

END OF ACT III.

ACT IV. SCENE II.

HAGAR'S TENT.

HAGAR.

Hagar.—What can mine anger do but burn within ?
It preys upon me. Do mine enemies
Feel for one moment but a spark from its flame ?
It was hurled forth with all my strength against
    them,
And from a greater height falls on my head !
What has my curse availed ? It was mere breath
Chased by the winds ! What is my hate to them ?
What is't but fire to water, whose moment's rage
Is hissed to blackness ?   It is some meteor
That idlers hardly gaze on, which may blaze
Unheeded in dull silence overhead ;
That is but seen to be smiled at; they will teach
A babe ere long to point his finger at it !
It is a poor caged beast that chafes with rage
But that its masters may more smile and triumph !
My son was yesterday the blessed heir
Of richest promises; his strength was dear;
His acts all doubled in his father's eye.
Now he's the servant of a poor weak babe,
An outcast from his father's heart; and I,
Who was but prized for his sake, with his fall

I am forgotten—the poor instrument,
When the object loses value must be flung away !
Enter ISHMAEL.
Ah, dearest son, blame not, but comfort me.
Alas, thou art despoiled, art cheated, tricked,
Robbed of thy right; a babe possesses it !   [talk,
Ishmael.—What mean you, mother? if of a babe you
    Sarah has borne a son.   My father's glad;
    I never saw him gladder.
Hagar.—   He smiles upon your death !
    You are now as one that's dead to him, my boy.
    You may boast of courage now; his favour's gone !
Ishmael.—I'll make it come again.   But have you heard.
    What preparation forward goes of his young men?
    They are all in arms !
Hagar.—   Have you heard why ?
    Is Abraham to lead them ?
Ishmael.—   No, and 'gainst whom
    They know not; they are something angered.
Hagar.—Know not 'gainst whom ?   'Tis not against
    your father ?
Ishmael.—No, 'tis to guard him from some other foe ;
    Eliezer set them on ; yet they complain.
    My father heads them not, that they must keep
    This arming secret from him; such was the word
    They had from Eliezer.
Hagar.—   'Tis most strange !
    They murmured then to you ?
Ishmael.—   Yes, and ere now

Have uttered such to me. In vain I tell them,
Think not I'll hear it. Speak not against my
    father.
Give me not praise that's more than mine to rob
Him of what justly is his due.
Hagar.—Son, listen to me. This was only right
As long as Abraham was kind to you,
And gave your due; but now he'll rob you of it,
Of praise and rights alike; for all is changed;
He is thine enemy : these men are thy friends.
Thou see'st they love thee still. Now list to me;
Put thyself at their head, recover thou
The rights that now slip from thee. Urge not love.
Thou art thy father's son no more. Obedience
Is only due to me, thy mother.
Ishmael.—   Mother, be sure
If there be some real enemy they know of,
And that my father will not fight against him,
Be assured that I, young as I am, will join them.
Hagar.—Suppose no enemy, or grant there be,
I tell thee none can be a greater one
Than Abraham.
Ishmael.—   My father, Abraham !
I will go straight and ask him what I have done.
He has forgiven me ere now, and tells me
Ever to speak out boldly to him.
Hagar.—   Thou wilt not understand !
Son, thou must fight against him, take from him
That which he holds !

Ishmael.—   Mother, I cannot do so.
One look of his would shame me.
Hagar.—   Thou foolish boy,
Has he not shamed thee more than this already ?
I tell thee he has robbed thee ; thou art nothing ;
And Sarah's son is everything.
Ishmael.—   Then if
I may but live with him and love him still ;
I'll make him love us both.   I'll love my
    brother.
Hagar.—And if thou dost thou hatest me, thy mother.
Now choose.—Sweet son, obey me ; 'tis but to go
And fight with thy dear friends, or not to fight,
And not against thy father.   'Tis but to arm
And ask him for thy own—he'll praise the deed,
And think thee brave ; 'tis meet thou shinest now,
Excelling in his eyes ; that babe will else
Snatch from thee all that thou hast won, and
    keep it.
Now join these youths, and say these words to
    them :—
' I come to join you ; we must from my father
Take some authority and wealth that's mine,
'Tis time I had my share, 'tis time, my friends,
That you had your just share of enterprise.'
Speak thus, act thus—thou win'st thy father's
    love
And thy companions'—do it not, thou losest all,
Any father's favour, mine, thy comrades'—all.

Ishmael.—Well, mother, I'll obey you ; 'tis my wish
As captain to lead forth my brave companions ;
My father keeps them p'rhaps too close at home ;
If you say he would love me for it after,
I'll do it.

Hagar.—Now about it, son ! I'll take thee with me ;
With me thou shalt address these brave young
men ;
'Twill win the love of all ; doubt not of it !

[Exeunt.

SCENE IV.

AN OPEN SPACE.

ABRAHAM—HAGAR—ISHMAEL.

Hagar.—You ask my reason. I'll not render it ;
If love reveal not this, think not that I
Will lead indifference to it. Ask the lioness
Robbed of her precious young, why she does
rage ;
Ask the cloud that's torn by the loud thunder why
It flashes angry lightning ; ask the sea
Lashed by the winds why it so gapes for ships ;
And if these answer not, will woman answer,
Why her fierce mischief follows her wrecked love ?

Think you that she will change your gentle
    coldness
By tame and humble answers into scorn?
Abraham.—Is this then woman's love? or wreck of
    love?
Can man's mere prudence she calls cold in-
    difference,
Urge her to mix in treasons 'gainst his life,
And be to him worse than an enemy?
Can she that once has loved her lord become
So basely treacherous?
Hagar.—   He has taken more than life—
Her pride, her peace, her happiness is gone!
What is her life to him; it is his scorn!
What is his death to her, if she too dies,
If both at last together rest in peace?
Abraham.—This is mere fury, and a poor excuse
For treason, which should meet with punishment.
Why should it not? As those poor instruments
That thou hast used have died, why should'st not
    thou
Die by a death more dreadful?
Hagar.—   Seek not now
To frighten me with threats : I care not for them;
Though from a tyrant, I have never feared thee;—
Alas, I loved thee ever!
Ishmael.—   Father, for me she speaks.
Anger her not, she thinks you love me not—
She is my mother ; how can I smile and see you

So vexing her? You love us not! nay, now
I'll anger you to have you rail on me.
Abraham.—Then, Ishmael, my child, tell calmly now,
What makes your mother so revengeful towards
me,
So fierce and bitter in her speech and look?
Ishmael.—It is now Sarah has a son, you say,
He must have rights you promised me; I none.
We think that your dear love is ebbing from
us;
We that did dance upon fresh laughing waves,
Are now left stranded, poor unsightly hulls.
Abraham.—Believe it not, my child! thou art as dear,
And as delightful to mine eye as when
I had no second son :—could I forget
My dear loved first-born? When have I seemed
Less loving, Ishmael? when have I shown
By any act, a wish that thou should'st lose
Thy rights?
Hagar.— Believe him not, my Ishmael;
For he has given me hopes much greater. Ah!
How sweet his smile; how the poor heart
before it
Can like a fool unlock its treasures. Rather,
How can a mouth that has framed such a smile
Not fear to be struck dumb at that word
treachery?
How can that smile enslave its beauty so
To be the liar of that shameless mouth!

L

Abraham.—Hagar, for shame ! thou heap'st up a dis-
    grace
    To teach this child to think of his father so.
Ishmael.—Mother, forbear.   I told you he was kind.
    I do believe him ; you are fierce with him.
    Forgive me !   He's my father ; look in his eyes,
    There is a soul of goodness in them.   He has
    promised.
    Then let us both be satisfied.
Hagar.—My lord, if you will grant one poor request,
    The last that Hagar offers thee, her heart
    Shall be as dead to treachery as love ;
    Give all the love, the favour that's my due,
    To this dear boy—let his life be as blest,
    As mine was wretched ; for my lavished love,
    Now give return to him, and I will bless thee
    As if for life I had been dearly loved,
    And mourned not as for worse than widowhood.
Abraham.—I understand not half thy bitter words,
    Thou ceasest not to pour them forth ; my love
    Thou art as scornful of as I was not,   [have it !
    As I have never been of thine ; thou wilt not
    Then gladly I must grant what thou has begged.
    Come, Ishmael, we two can love as friends,
    And both still love thy mother, she will p'r'aps
    Love us the more if we look not upon her,
    If we speak kindly to her she but answers
    With angry speeches, we will talk together,
    While she speaks still to the winds.

Hagar.—   You mock me still ;
How easy when the heart is cold to mock !
How hard while it still glows to keep from rage
At hearing such dire cruelty—rage 'gainst itself
For having weakened its own self for such.
But I will bear it all. I say my heart
Is dead to love or hate, if thou wilt love
In that full measure due to me, this boy.

*Ishmael.—*Mother, he has said he would ; why do you
    still
Speak with such anger to him? Be at peace :
Embrace him as I do !

Hagar.—   Embrace thou him for me.
I am at peace with him if he now do
The like to thee.

*Abraham (embracing Ishmael).—*Yes, thus I end all
    discord,
And Hagar, if sweet childhood take thy love,
Thy love should to itself take some sweet child-
    hood.   [*Exeunt.*

SCENE V.

A TENT.

SARAH—ELIEZER—SARAH *lying on a bed.*

*Eliezer.—*Madam, I saw my master Abraham
Dismiss his armed protectors—they are gone.

The way lies free to King Abimelech;
And you are stolen again ; unless, I say,
Unless you could alarm your lord, and make him
(As I could not) look to his safety.
Sarah.—   I said before,
And say again, my lord may seem unwise,
But to do more, were faithlessness in God;
God did protect us so and fight for us
When King Abimelech first came on us,
That you, and all may rest in faith assured,
He ne'er will tempt again our champion.
Eliezer.—Ay, madam, yet may not his shame
Be stronger than his fear ; may not you trust
Unwarrantably in a Providence
That gives most help to those that help them-
    selves ;
'Tis scorn of instruments through which he works,
That he allows to work, if, when these are urged,
As they are now, with the like we fight not too.
What potent means are now in use against you !
Think, with what subtle tongue, this Hagar's
    maid
Will paint your beauty and your yielding weak-
    ness !
Imputing vice to raise your value more
In his vice-loving eyes, which prompts his heart,
And shames his mind to make a second raid !
Sarah.—Let her but try ! she draws down death upon
    her—

Her mistress too, deserves no less—but thou,
If thou malignest King Abimelech,
And thus distrustest so God's providence,
Wilt draw on thine own head a punishment
No less accursed—begone, why camest thou
To trouble me with tricks and poor designs
Of wicked, God-forgetting women? art thou of
 them?—
Know then that God gives to the course of time,
To bring their plans to ridicule, themselves
To punishment.

Eliezer.—   Madam, I do entreat you,
Call not the faithful watch who gives alarm,
Or him who cries at sight of coming danger,
The thief and the assailant ; if my care
Has been suspicious fearfulness—my eyes
Seeing my fancies, pardon me ! but this at worst
Is being forewarned—the zeal if over-zeal
Incurs no feverish danger-haste, but only
Impatience without danger.

Sarah.—   Why all this talk ?
I ask thee, Art thou of them ? say at once,
I am not—and not of their company,
Be not so full of their thoughts, now go !
For I would rest with this sweet babe beside me.
O that thou hadst the faith in God that we have !
God, open this man's eyes as Thou hast ours !
And open this man's heart as Thou hast ours !
            [*Sleeps.*

Eliezer.—She sleeps. Well, this is all my alarming
and danger-crying brings. I'll say no more and let
the danger come; it may be as they say, that
God protects them, and if so God protects me
from disgrace too. What a trembling she gave
me when she said, 'Are you of them,' yet she
knows nothing. Well, if I only run more risk by
giving the alarm than by keeping silent, I'll keep
silent. Whatever comes I have given full warning.

[*Exit* ELIEZER.

END OF ACT IV.

ACT V. SCENE I.

TABLES SPREAD UNDER THE SHADE OF TREES.

ABRAHAM—KING ABIMELECH—ANER—ESCHOL—
MAMRE—THEIR SONS—YOUNG MEN, SERVANTS, &C.
—SARAH—HAGAR—THEIR WIVES, MAID-SERVANTS,
&c., *waiting on them.*

Aner (aside to Eschol and Mamre).—How royal is this
    feast ; how royally
Does Abraham become the table ; how his eye
Beams with a welcome round !—'tis bright as
    youth's ;
His wrinkles hid with smiles ; he looks as fresh
As from that conquest that we three did share in
(Now many a year ago), his manhood came.
Eschol (aside to Aner and Mamre).—Yes, should a
    stranger now behold the two,
If he were told one was a king, the other
At first a shepherd, now with richest flocks,
A dweller still in tents—which would he crown ?
Mamre (aside to Aner and Eschol).—He'd say the
    man who eyed his questioner
With such full glances, who looked up so boldly,

And spoke so calmly forth his well-weighed
   words,
Was certainly the king. That he, saying naught,
Who scarce looks up, but listens with bowed
   head,
Is one who counts and counts again his wealth,
Viewing his flocks, conversing but with shepherds.
Aner (*aside to Eschol and Mamre*).—The wonder's
   greater when you know our friend
Has never deigned to count : on that great day,
You both know how for each of us he laid
Sure wealth on wide foundation, from his own
Plucked the foundation laid.
Abraham.—What talk you of so earnestly, my three
Tried and most dear associates in arms?
Does thought of that great day, or my as great
And later blessing sober you?
Aner.—My brother, we were wondering, as we called
The past again to view, how it should happen,
That you who robbed yourself and made us rich,
Should after lingering so outstrip us all,
And win a wealth, that is as great as this
Your present happiness!
Eschol.—What is your secret, brother? you can spare it.
What is the talisman, the charm, the watch-word,
Has made you able to go in and out,
'Mongst jealous heathen foes still journeying on,
Your wealth so poorly guarded, it would seem
A bribe to thieves to steal it.

Abraham.—I marvel you should ask who fought with
 me;
And who now see a son born to my age.
 (*Turning to* King Abimelech.)
The King Abimelech, my greater, he
Can tell you that no greatness is in me,
That he so prosperous now could stoop to lying !
So valiantly as he once fought with you,
Yet from suspicion only of mere strangers,
With coward fear could cling to baser falsehood.
Was't not so?

Abimelech.—And if it were so, what small lapse it was
Of pardonable weakness—hide it rather.
You wrong yourself, my brother; all who hear you
Must magnify your fault; for who would think
With this grave speech of yours 'tis what it is,
A theme for gentle laughter—but your pardon !
I see you are angry.

Abraham.—   No, you've made me sad,
And on this day when I thought nothing could.
I am in these men's eyes so lifted up,
That they give me God's glory. I bade thee
To prove me nothing; thou hast raised me
 higher,
Making my glory falser, God's left hid.
How I must tremble when I pray to Him ;
Lest thankless for this blessing, for this wealth,
This gracious promise now fulfilled to me,
And safe prosperity 'midst enemies,

I too call faithlessness a lapse, a weakness,
So pardonably human; thus you called it.
Yet that sin struck at all my happiness,
For it was doubt, denial of this favour,
His promises and His kind providence,
To whom I owed all wealth, success, and peace,
That then were mine—such ample proofs of love!
Talk no more lightly of it—Sarah, come,
Tell all of us to whom thou ow'st this blessing
To have a son in thine old age ; say now,
What faith it gives to thee.

Sarah.—My lord, and my lord's friends, all you who
    hear me,
Rejoice with me, for God hath made me to laugh !
Give Him the glory, look with solemn faces,
With slowly moving lips speak out your praise
To this wide heaven whence such blessing flows.
But laugh with me, and look with radiant smiles
Into my eyes that triumph. Who would have said
That Sarah in old age should bear a son !
Yet see, I yesterday did wean the child,
From whom the seed that's promised is to spring.
Who now will doubt God's promises ? How
    foolish,
How wicked was I doubting all would be
In me fulfilled !

Ishmael (aside to Hagar).—Is she not foolish now ?
Doubting that in myself there is fulfilled
All promise ; this she boasts of is but more,

And larger measure, why so much on it?
Why do they look so grave? I will laugh for them
(SARAH *sees* ISHMAEL *laughing and looks angrily at him.*)
Tell them, my mother, thou hadst better cause
To laugh at God's fulfilment!

Hagar (aside to Ishmael).— Hush, my son!
Thy father called her; 'tis his policy now
To let her boast 'fore great and many friends.
(*Aside.*) Yet I fear for thee, he makes too much of it.

Abraham.—Wife, wherefore so pale? this day's too
    much for thee.
This blessing overpowers—what, still worse?
Conduct her to my tent; all you my friends,
Disperse now, leave us to our peaceful quiet.
Great joys are dangerous as greatest griefs,
And blessings borne not humbly turn to curses;
We added your rich kindness and now groan
Beneath our treasures' load.   [*rest*

Abimelech.—Farewell, my brother, may God's blessing
    On you and Sarah.

Aner.—Brother, farewell, I carry blessing from you
    In righteous wise instruction.

Eschol.—With kindest farewell, I too thank you
    brother—
The secret of the King of kings is with you.

Mamre.—Farewell, dear brother, I have learnt from
    thee
That looking heavenwards gives the kingly mien.
                                    [*Exeunt.*

SCENE II.

HAGAR'S TENT.

HAGAR *and* ELIEZER.

Hagar.—Did Abraham then give the smallest way
,   To Sarah's wildness, to her senseless folly?
Eliezer.—At first he would not, said he had promised you
To show that loving favour to his first-born
He had shown before.
Hagar.—   And did he change from this?
Eliezer.—He did, when solemnly she spake these words,
'Cast out the bondwoman; her son shall not
Be heir with the son of the free.' At this he changed;
Yet left her saying that he could not.
Hagar.   Heartless wretch!—
Why did he not cast her out; he was tame!
Why should he let her tongue run on against us!
Eliezer.—Hagar, howe'er this be, take my advice—
Tempt not thy fortune further. What if he change?
He may side with her. Wait not thou for it!
Hagar.—I will not wait!—I'll end this wretched strife

And make him swear 'fore God, in God's own
 name,
In Sarah's presence too what he has promised.
She then shall know herself to be a devil,
If she should tempt him break his oath to God!
Eliezer.—Believe me, he will never swear so much.
 I saw how much he changed. Do not hope this.
 Do anything but this.
Hagar.—   What would'st thou have me do?
Eliezer.—Go forth with Ishmael; I will furnish you.
 In ending strife you call his blessing on you,
 His help, and his protection; but opposing
 What certain must befall, you get disgrace,
 Contempt, and unhelped banishment.
Hagar.—Think'st thou that all are coward slaves as
 thou art!
 Think'st thou that all are base in mind as thou
 art!
 Could Sarah bring disgrace on me though thou
 Should'st help her devilry with cunning? Dar'st
 thou
 Upon thy master heap this vile abuse?
 Begone, or I shall tear out that base tongue that
 spake it,
 And stab to the heart that framed it, spill its dregs,
 And with the filthy channels that conveyed it.
         [*Exit* ELIEZER.

Contaminate the winds!—'Tis well thou'rt gone!
I would not stain my hands with blood of man.

It is not true!—he trembled as he told it;
Seeing her rage he thought my lord must be
As fearful and as wickedly unjust
As he would be—he has no sense of truth,
And his poor, false mind yields at the first assault
Of malice and strong lying.   Why advise it?
Why should he speak this to me?—'tis himself
To free from all suspicion.   He does fear
Lest I revive conspiracy, or the old
Be traced in part to him.—O traitor! worse!
O wretch unfeeling who for coward-safety,
When nothing threatens would'st betray thy friends
To misery and death!—O my sweet son!
What wild beasts lurk around thy innocence!
Whose treacherous-cruel and base savagery
Would drown in blood thy beauty—wretched envy
Spurring to malice so their blind brute-fury
That rage would live much longer than thy life,
And without light be trampling still; but know,
And let thy tenderness, sweet boy, take courage,
Thy parents shame their glare, and can appal
     them
With watch of truthful eyes; they durst not come
One poor step farther, though at the bound they
     came,
Winged with their hate and hateful jealousies,
With rankling malice galling their base hearts—
No more!—I give them thought and words too
     many.

If for eternity live truth and right
These insects of an hour are not worth anger;
I will go forth and cool the blood a little,
This viper's sting has heated; long before
I should have crushed it crawling, with my heel.

[*Exit* HAGAR.

SCENE III.

A HILL-SIDE, TOWARDS EVENING.

Two SHEPHERDS.

1*st Old Shepherd.*—Didst thou see the king, man, and
his young men, how bravely they came to the
feast and went away again—all mounted? It was
a brave sight!

2*nd Old Shepherd.*—Ay, that did I, brother, I marvelled
he should bring such show to our valley; but our
master need not fear him; our master's wiser
than he, for all his show!

1*st Old Shepherd.*—I was minded to run down to him
through them all and kneel down to him for my
son—my poor son, though they say he is dead.

2*nd Old Shepherd.*—That he is most certain; you had
got nothing by this, brother, it would have angered
him, no more.

1st Old Shepherd.—Yet when I saw all those brave youths, I thought, why could not my son be amongst them ; he was a strong lad !—he wanted to rise !—he would have risen if he had lived. Why couldn't he live ? What fear had King Abimelech of him with all those lads around him ?

2nd Old Shepherd.—Why, dost not see ? King Abimelech did not kill him for himself, but for our master's sake ; the fear he has for our master made him kill thy son, as it made him make this show to day. Our master prospers—let all who wish to prosper too say, ' Good ! ' to it—if any say, ' I will prosper more,' or, 'He shall not prosper'—the word's enough—he dies—thy son said this, he died—thou didst half say it, thou wast nearly dead—is this not so ?

1st Old Shepherd.—Yes, yes, I know it, brother, yet 'tis hard. I would our master prospered and yet that I had not lost my son. I find his service hard ; for I must give my strength and give my son too, for food and clothing.

2nd Old Shepherd.—Thou'd'st better tell him so !— see, here he comes !

1st Old Shepherd.—No, no, I do unsay it—speak not thou of it.

[*Enter* ABRAHAM.

2nd Old Shepherd.—God's blessing on you, master ; to your sons

Your blessing and prosperity for a life
As long as yours !

Abraham.—God's blessing rest upon you both—I pray
you,
Has either seen my son, young Ishmael ?

2*nd Old Shepherd.*—I have not seen him, master.

1*st Old Shepherd.*— I have neither.

Abraham.—Go each of you a different way, and seek
him.
Send him to me ; I stay here till he comes—

[*Exeunt* SHEPHERDS.

To tell him what ?—to tell him he has lost
A father, I have lost a son. O God
Prompt me to speak it gently ! Thou hast
laid
This bitter task upon me ; lighten it,
That it swell not his heart as mine ; or hide,
Hide his face from me, blind my vision to it ;
Let me like lightning strike and vanish ; make
His child-heart rocky and defiant as a man's !
Soften his mother's rage ; as to a storm
That sweeps inevitable may she bend.
Give him an angel's eloquence to win her ;
Fill up her void of love with thine, and banish
For ever from her breast her direst foe,
Mad headstrong jealousy.

[*Enter* ISHMAEL.

Ishmael.—O father, I sought everywhere to find
you :

M

I have a favour I must ask of you.
I'm glad to find you here alone.
Abraham.—What is it, Ishmael ?   God grant that it be
Something thy father Abraham can grant !
Ishmael.—I have ta'en you in ill time ; I see you are
grave ;
But I must speak it, or perhaps occasion
May never serve again.
Abraham.—   It may not—speak !
Ishmael.—This day at the feast when all was joyousness,
And I was joyful, jesting with companions—
We listened not, nor heard your serious talk ;
We looked not on your faces till you drew
Both eyes and ears by calling loud for Sarah.
She then as loudly and with moving gesture
Spoke forth her happiness and praised its Giver.
I heard her solemn words, but seriousness
Seemed to me then mere sport and mockery.
I doubted too their import ; she gave praise
For one son, not for me the other ; this
I whispered laughing to my mother Hagar.
'Twas then a glance of fierceness fell on me
Darted from Sarah's eyes, falling on mine,
That careless gazed with blinding lightning-flash.
This weighted my light heart, and stilled my
mirth
As thunder silences the singing birds.
I come now, father, and confess my fault ;
And ask for thy forgiveness ; then that thou

Should'st beg forgiveness for the fault confessed
From Sarah.

Abraham.— Yes, I forgive thee. O my son,
Why com'st thou now to show more grace, and
    win
More love, to give more pain in pleasing so !

Ishmael.—Yes, I am sure of your love, my dear father ;
But not so sure of Sarah's—speak to her for me.

Abraham (*aside*).—'Tis time I tell him all.

(*Aloud.*) Listen to me, my son, speak not the while ;
'Twill pain thee now to hear what I must say ;
But answer not—each word's a grief to speak ;
Make me speak no word twice, and stay me not
To think on what I am speaking—'Tis not Sarah—
Think not her wishes wrong thee—God has
    spoken ;
I am His messenger to thee and Hagar—
Thy mother and thyself must leave me—answer
    not !
Thou art my firstborn, truly, but my son
No less by a bond-woman—Sarah's son
Is son of a free-woman—he must be my heir,
By staying here thou would'st be his co-heir.
This cannot be, for God has spoken it,
Confirming Sarah's words. Look not so sad !
This blessing's left thee, thou too art an heir
Of promises—God hath told me thine
Shall be a mighty race ; thy name shall live ;
Thyself be honoured through all future ages.

This exile shall at first seem hard; yet doubt not
Thy life's preserved for greatness. O my son,
God's love and mine shall ever follow thee !
Now go to Hagar—as the Lord sent me,
Say I sent thee. May-be He speaks again,
In this dread hour when I much need His
    comfort.

> [*Exit* ISHMAEL.
> [*After some time exit* ABRAHAM.

SCENE IV.

AN OPEN SPACE NEAR THE TENTS—ELIEZER AND
YOUNG MEN.

ISHMAEL *coming out alone meets* ABRAHAM *carrying
a leathern water-bottle.*

Abraham.—God's blessing on thee, dearest Ishmael ;
    where
Is Hagar ?   Did you give my message, Eliezer ?
Eliezer.—I did, my lord, but she would scarcely hear it—
Called it a lie.
Abraham.—Where is she, Ishmael?   Wherefore comes
    she not ?
Ishmael.—Father, she will not come till I return,
And say I must depart and you are here.

Abraham.—Then go and tell it her. Why are these
here? [*To* ELIEZER.
[*Exit* ISHMAEL.
Eliezer.—They heard her clamour, and had fears lest
Hagar
Did meditate some violence.
Abraham.—Well, they are faithful, but not too kind
servants.

Enter SARAH.

Wife, wherefore are you come?
Sarah.—I come to give a parting word of kindness,
To show poor Hagar I forgive her angers,
To mingle with the blessings you bestow
My word of prayer and comfort.

Enter ISHMAEL *followed by* HAGAR, *looking down.*

Abraham.—Hagar, you've heard my message, and
have heard [leave us;
God's message too. I mourn that you must
But you must journey towards the desert Paran;
Both Sarah, I, and all of us have come
To call God's blessing on you. I will bind
This vessel on you to preserve your lives;
'Twill save from thirst, God will provide the rest.

HAGAR *looks not on him, and moves away when he goes
to bind the bottle upon her.*

What mean you Hagar, still to disobey
Both God's commands and mine! Oh make not
harder
The task God wills, and I must execute;

Enough, it is His positive command.
Now, pain us not by what is useless rage!
Hagar.—Son, speak again, and tell him first, I speak
Not once more to him if I go or stay.
But say, wilt thou yield tame obedience,
And see thy birthright thus snatched from thee by
This weakest trickery and this wretched babe?
Sarah.—Thou swarthy slave, what right hast thou to
    speak
So vilely of this free-born child of mine?
Abraham.—Peace, Sarah! let her go with blessing; 'tis
    her rage
That tempests in her when she speaks against us!
Hagar.—I wait to hear you speak, my son.   I scorn
To speak one word to her, and of her babe.
I'll never speak again.   Now kill and banish
Me thy own mother with one word, or prove
Thou art a man and her most dear-loved son!
Abraham.—Stay, son, speak not; this is too cruel for
    thee.
Hagar, now wrath is cruel to your son;
See, how your anger blinds!—He shall not answer!
Your death and banishment shall never seem
To hang upon his word!   Now go,
Wait not his answer, only hear my blessing!
Hagar.—Ishmael's made dumb!   My son is over-
    awed.
Both Abraham and Sarah now may kill,   [not!
Or curse me dead.   I go not!   Ishmael bids me

Young Men.—We said she would not, never will
 she go !

Eliezer.—Young men, be ready all against the signal.
 Then seize and bind her ! She must be carried
 hence.

Abraham.—Who must be seized, thou agéd cruelty ?
 Young men, I do command you, bind Eliezer,
 Carry him hence, and go with him yourselves !
 We need not this officious championship.

　　　　　[*Exeunt* YOUNG MEN *with* ELIEZER.
 Now Hagar, take my blessing, then depart
 At once with Ishmael. Hear again what God
 Has promised thee, to cheer thy banishment.
 At first this must be grievous, why I know not ;
 But trial will o'ertake thee in the desert.
 To try thy faith, in what great blessing follows,
 This sweet child like a fading flower shall sicken,
 He shall seem dying ; thou awhile shalt leave him,
 Thy sad heart agonized to see the sight,
 Not daring to look on it. Then an angel
 Shall come to thee and bid thee rise and look.
 From that same hour, as if this angel gave it,
 Thy dear-loved Ishmael shall be blessed ; the
 hand
 Of God shall be with him. He shall become
 A mighty archer, brave and skilled in fight,
 The hand of every man against him, his
 Stronger than every man's ; the founder of
 A mighty race, who shall great cities build,

Possessors of high arts, of light, of knowledge,
That then shall shine when all the world around
Is sunk in barbarous ignorance ; this shall hand
His name and honour down to distant ages.
This child thou see'st, to him shall generations
Through the long centuries of years look back,
In him behold their great progenitor.   [son.
Now take my blessing with you. Kiss me, my
May God in heaven bless both you and Hagar ;
And keep you, looking on you lovingly,
As I have done ; but more than I could do ;
With everlasting eyes, untiring guardianship ;
Sweet boy, a last farewell to you and Hagar !

Sarah.—My blessing on you both, and free forgiveness
Of all against myself ; this kiss to thee,
Young Ishmael, heir to all these blessed promises,
A kind farewell to you and Hagar !

Ishmael.—Farewell to you, dear father; farewell to you,
Dear Sarah ; may God's blessing rest on you,
As I believe His blessing rests on me !

ABRAHAM *binds the bottle on* HAGAR, *who slowly
follows* ISHMAEL.

[*Exeunt* ABRAHAM *and* SARAH.

END OF ACT V.

FINIS.

A Dramatic Sketch

CALLED

'RAVENSWOOD.'

INTRODUCTION.

THIS 'dramatic sketch' is founded on the story of Scott's well-known novel 'The Bride of Lammermoor.' I made what use I could of all the characters, but was obliged to omit the comic ones and to supply their place by very solemn and serious allegorical names, which I hope I have redeemed from the coldness and meagreness that they generally imply.

The pathetic story is known to most readers, but a brief outline may be of service :

The father of Lord Edgar Ravenswood was at one time possessed of all the estates that at the beginning of Scott's story were the property of Sir William Ashton. There was naturally very bitter feeling between the two families, the property having changed hands chiefly for party reasons and by confiscation. An old family had been ruined and an upstart family enjoyed their wealth. Lord Edgar inherited this hate and a wretched remnant of the property called Wolf's Crag. But love is the strongest of all the passions, and the beauty of Lucy Ashton charmed away his feelings of revenge. The affection was returned—the young nobleman was handsome and had saved her life. All might have ended peacefully, but for the jealousy and prejudice of one person, Lady Ashton. This woman lost all motherly feeling, and though

she knew how completely her daughter's affections were
engaged, she did not scruple to coerce her, even at the risk of
health and reason. Such devilry will pride sometimes prompt
a heart to ! It ended in the complete overthrow of the poor
girl's mind, under circumstances horrible enough. She had
married the man her mother forced upon her ; but on the
first night after the wedding, while all were dancing and
enjoying themselves, shrieks were heard coming from the
bridal chamber. The room was burst open and the wife was
found a laughing maniac, with the husband stabbed to the
heart lying on the bed. Ravenswood himself is represented
by Scott as having been necessarily delayed abroad, and, all
letters being intercepted by Lady Ashton's precautions, as
having heard nothing. At last one message from his lover
did reach him, and he returned just in time to find her married
to another. The scene of proud defiance and terrible earnest-
ness where he faces all the family, reproaches poor Lucy
Ashton, and restores the pledge of her engagement, is painted
with all the power of Scott's genius, and must be referred to
by the reader, since it was impossible to reproduce it in this
play. His death followed early on the next day, so that these
lovers died within perhaps six hours of each other. Riding
by a shorter way along the shore to keep his appointment for
a duel with Colonel Ashton, it is nearly certain he was
engulfed, horse and all, in a quicksand. Only a plume was
found near the spot where he had last been seen. This is
typical of what is left of the pride and wealth of these families
—only a beautiful yet terrible romance ; at the same time,
one which may cause them never to be forgotten.

DRAMATIS PERSONÆ.

Sir William Ashton.
Lord Edgar Ravenswood.
Hayston of Bucklaw.
Captain Craigengelt.
Caleb Balderstone.
Colonel Douglas Ashton.
Charles Edward Stuart.
A Chaplain.
A Lawyer.
Two French Soldiers.
Lady Ashton.
Lucy Ashton, her daughter.
Mrs. Douglas Ashton.
A Nurse.
Old Alice.
Ailsie Gourlay.
Annie Winnie.

Revenge.	Swearing.	Charity.
Charon.	Drunkenness.	Temperance.
Despair.	The Seven	Simplicity.
Destruction.	Deadly Sins.	Purity.
Discord.	Evil Spirits.	Truth.
Malice.	Honour.	Fame.
Spite.	Courage.	Peace.
Famine.	Faith.	Concord.
Murder.	Hope.	Fairies.

.•

ACT I. SCENE I.

INTERIOR OF A COTTAGE AT NIGHT.

*By a brazier of coals burning low—*OLD ALICE—
AILSIE GOURLAY—ANNIE WINNIE.

Alice.—What charm did'st utter while thou gav'st his
    lips
Herb aconitum with nine others 'stilled?
Ailsie.—Keep the soul, through body go,
Thus permit the Powers below.
Alice.—This hour he's slept, his soul at peace, but now
He frowns and mutters—who is by him?—who?
Annie.—   You said his chaplain.
Alice.—   Ask not of him. He spoke,
But I could hear no words.
Annie.—   They were, ' Forgive,
Or take no sacrament.'
Alice.—   His answer was,
' I will repent but ne'er forgive ; he is
My enemy in death.' The chaplain's gone—
Who kneels?
Annie.—   His son! I'm deaf to what they speak.

Ailsie.—The flame leaps in this brazier ; 'tis my drug
    Kindles afresh his life.

Alice.—   It gives his soul
    Fuel for one bright highest flicker, to last
    While I am speaking of it.   He is strong
    To sit up straight in bed ; he stretches hands—
    Both hands, and searches with them—there !
    Both now are resting on his son's bowed head ;
    His eyes gleam bright as frost-surrounded fires,
    As thus he screams and whispers, ' Son,
    ' I can bequeath no patrimony, lands
    ' I had but have not.   I bequeath my curse.
    ' Cut off this lock of hair, cut one of thine.'
    The youth has taken two. ' Now fling them both
    ' Upon those blazing coals.   Now kneel again.
    ' As those two locks have shrivelled and are
        naught,
    ' So wilt thou hunt till they are naught—if this
    ' My curse thou should'st fulfil—the lives of his
    ' And him who robbed me, cheated me of mine,
    ' Disgraced my house, degraded my great name.
    ' Not in the field of fight by violence
    ' He snatched all from me, but by creeping guile.
    ' Think him more base for this, not kinder ; tread
    ' His life out like a scorpion's ; but not yet,
    ' Not yet !—abide your time ; and when you strike,
    ' Strike sure.   My strength is going, my curse
    ' Dies on my lips—let your lips speak it till
    ' 'Tis done ; whisper it daily till——'

Annie.—   This flame
Sinks in white ashes !

Alice.—   He is ashes now.
Come, you are wanted to lay out his corpse.
I'll go and take some rest ; lead my blind steps !
Lo, I am in this dark real world again.
Go you, I know my cottage ; reach my crutch !

                              [*Exeunt.*

SCENE II.

WOLF'S CRAG—A CHAMBER.

LORD EDGAR RAVENSWOOD—CHAPLAIN.

Ravenswood.—Then we must lose you, sir.   It grieves
    me much.
You have been my father's friend, my boyhood's
    friend.
Alas, my means may not reward a service,
Holy and necessary and faithful too.

Chaplain.—   But that
No private means of mine are by to feed
Those that pertain to me, I would, my lord,
Die in your service, and perform the rites
Daily in this your chapel which have been
By me these twenty years performed : to leave it

Is such a grief to me, my wife, and children,
That high'st preferment should not lure us, only
Dire necessity like that now speaks.
Ravenswood.—   You leave
A district poorer for your going; now
May sour and insolent presbyters yet more
Lord it—while you remained this air we breathe
Was purer.
Chaplain.—   By their fruits you know them; as
Their greed for money, their base faith, was shown
In that betrayal of King Charles, the fruit
Corrupt and bitter of hypocrisy,
Which yet professes to religion's name—
So was this taint apparent in to-day's
So heartless interruption ; when all eyes
Should have been weeping, and all mouths
Dumb with true reverence and sorrow—then
To stare on us and bawl forth claims of law !
See, my lord, these are they who in their chapels
Will push for precedence and hour-long wrangle.
        Enter CALEB BALDERSTONE.
Caleb.—My lord, your guests demand more wine.
Ravenswood.—   Give't, then !
You keep the cellar, give it them.
Caleb.—   We have
The newer that was to be kept a year ;
The old is drunk—must they have two years'
        share ?
*Ravenswood.—*Ay, or two more.   Go, give it them.

Caleb.—   We have
But two years' fair supply.

Ravenswood.—   Empty the cellar, go;
We'll try and fill't again.

Caleb.—   My lord, to-morrow
It could be filled.   I only urge convenience ;
Might we not have new guests too soon to-
    morrow ?

Ravenswood.—You shall lose your office, Caleb—serve
    your guests.
Are you a butler to neglect them ?—go !
                        [*Pushes him out.*
This faithful wretch so clings to my poor
    fortunes,
He'll swear they flourish still.

(*A burst of revelry heard.*)   And that sounds like it !
How often have the walls of yonder castle
Listened to merriment like that, when bold
And loyal soldier-hearts beat fervently
To acclamations that their strong voice uttered,
One of my ancestors speaking to their eyes
And ears, the man whom they had followed
To the hunt or fight, and seen him ever foremost,
First in the sport, the boldest of bold horsemen,
Whose merry laugh came floating back to them ;
Or in the field as gay on charger heading
Their troop through the hail of bullets, fighting on
Against the king—then woe to that king !—or
    with him.

After this chase or fight, the end the same,
With feasting, merriment, quaffing to the dead,
Toasting the living, they at the castle gathered ;
There would laugh over, telling of the scrambles,
The scratches got, or laugh as much to speak
Of deadly spear-thrusts, seen a moment ere
They drank the heart's blood, seen not soon
    enough
To push quite past a limb or finger. This
Would be talk for men ; but ladies were then
    cheered,
Talked to as lovingly, with courtesy
As gentle by these warriors, whose reward
Was to receive sweet smiles in their true hearts.
The dance would then answer to music's sound.
Youth would give promise of exploits to beauty
Great as his love, and beauty generously
Would fire the youths by graciousness to deeds
Great as were his who'd won the bride, whom
    you,
Your father, or a grandsire had bade honour
The honourable hero on that day.
Chaplain.—I do remember to have joined a lady
Unto a princely man, your father's cousin.
What a fairy was she ! how all faces seemed
On that night doubly lighted, by keen joy,
Then by the torches' shining on bright glitter,
Dresses, and gold, and diamonds !—how the
    walls

N

That rang with music, how the floor that
trembled
Beneath the pulse of feet, seemed to be moving !
One as its tapestry were living, and the floor
As if it were a sea with bright glad waves.
My eyes swam then to look on what my heart
So thrilled ; they swim now thinking on't.

Ravenswood.—When scenes like this, and many a scene
as noble,
Have been the history, happy, chequered, sad,
Of one great family, is there not some right
To keep the great stage for that family ?
May other baser ones inhabit rooms,
And tread the walks all sacred to us, to
Some joy or woe of one of our great name ?
These spots heard hallowed words or saw such
looks
As frenzied the beholders—is it, then,
Less of a sacrilege for baser natures
To tenant here than lie dead in our tombs ?

Enter a LORD.

Lord.—Come, Ravenswood, why mourn so much the
dead ? We want your presence.

Ravenswood.—I'll follow you.   Farewell !   And let
me oft hear of you.   [*To* CHAPLAIN.

Chaplain.—Farewell, my lord !

[*Exit* CHAPLAIN.

Lord.—We're hatching a sweet plan. This is it. If
you lead on we'll follow and clear the Lord

Keeper out of your castle. We'll fight, my lord, as we fought for your father. What say you to't?

Ravensuood.—I don't wish for braver fellows. To-morrow we'll think over it and be steady too.

Lord.—Steady we are not; give me your arm, my lord.

[*Exeunt.*

SCENE III.

A TERRACE WALK. ON A SEAT.

LUCY ASHTON—NURSE.

Nurse.—Bless you, dear, you have a sweet voice. I said you would have when you cried so prettily as a baby. It shall win you a fine husband soon, and then I may go. But I shall never be happy till I see you married.

Lucy.—Have I improved so much? I think it is the sweet songs more than the dull teaching. Will you hear another, Nurse?

Nurse.—Ay, to be sure I will; they cheer my old ears; though there is a story of a poor lady—she was perhaps your years, dear—there was one song she sang plaintively.

Lucy.—Only one song?

Nurse.—You shall hear why—It was the song her
lover taught her and his favourite one; so when
he left her—

Lucy.—Did he leave her—oh, why?

Nurse.—He left to join his regiment, which was in
France, and this song she sang to sweeten her
memory of him—she would sing it every evening;
and if company were at the castle they liked to
hear her sing it.

Lucy.—Because she sang it better than any one else
could.

Nurse.—She sang it with a melting sweetness; so that
all who heard her could not help weeping.

Lucy.—Did she weep?   [weep.

Nurse.—I did not say she wept; but she made others

Lucy.—And did he return and marry her?

Nurse.—No, there is the sadness of it. One evening
she was singing this song, and she seemed to sing
with such power—oh, so beautifully! and yet
wildly; as you shall see—for when the last note
was done, she did not sit down, and all had started
to their feet hearing her sing so—well, past them
all she darted towards the open window—for it
was summer—leapt out, and ran over the terrace,
as it might be here—

Lucy.—Oh, Nurse, what did she mean?

Nurse.—Why, the poor thing had gone mad. When
the gentlemen an hour later came up to her she
was mad!

Lucy.—Oh, how dreadful! But what made her so,
Nurse?

Nurse.—Her lover had that moment broken his vow.
They heard by the next ship that he had married
a noble lady in France.

Lucy.—Poor, poor, lady! But the wickedness of that
man! My song, I see, may be very sad, when I
thought it only pretty.

Nurse.—Now sing it, dear.

Lucy sings.—Ye flowers fresh that garland May,
Ye fires on summer skies that play;
The waters laugh; the leaves have stirred
To hear your love-chant, singing bird.

I wander 'mongst the beechen shade,
And tread where sunny beams have strayed;
For here where once I heard her talk
I with her spirit seem to walk.

She is no spirit, were she so
How sweet through death to her to go!
Oh! smile not skies, but frown as when
They thundered, 'Never come again.'

' Never on peril of your life! '
Ye shades may see a bloody strife !—
Yet lull me, say they will not come,
That she alone your paths will roam.

Wave every branch! and sing out clear,
Sweet birds, when sweeter sounds ye hear;

And where her footsteps glide your grace,
Ye ferns and trees in fresh founts trace.

But if she comes not, summer fly ;
Ye leaves and birds, ye flowers, die ;
Let winter crash the forest drear,
And drown with floods, with lightning sear !

Nurse.—I should love you for singing so, dear, if I
were a young man.   But come, it has made you
pale; we must quicken those roses to life again.

[*Exeunt.*

SCENE IV.

A LIBRARY AT RAVENSWOOD CASTLE.

SIR W. ASHTON—A LAWYER.

Lawyer.—The scene was as I've told it ; I was seized,
Pinioned and twenty swords were at my throat ;
And this for bidding them desist from forms
Popish and traitorous, showing my warrant from
you.
Sir William.—And having silenced you, the prayers
were read,
The   surpliced   clergyman   with   prayer-book
standing,
And all engaging with him in it ?

Lawyer.—All this was done, Sir William; but worse
    follows.
    The ceremony o'er, these gentlemen
    Listened, while he who calls himself The Master,
    Addressed a speech inflaming them to anger
    'Gainst you and me your messenger; he said,
    ' Bailiffs and ruffians, but for your drawn swords,
    ' Most kind and noble kinsmen, had this day
    ' Prevented the due rites of burial to
    ' My father. Thanks to you, noble friends; I feel
    ' Strong to oppose his malice who has dug,
    ' And meanly now disturbs this grave. Know well
    ' I will requite such insult on him, or may I
    ' Be driven by him to my grave, and be
    ' Molested thus in it.' He said this speech,
    And all with gesture threatening, murmur deep,
    Applauded what he said. This done, all go
    And feast the evening at his tower. I there
    Gleaned through some waiting-men, they spoke
        and pledged
    Vows of a murderous violence towards you.
    Now take your measures, sir, for certainly
    These knaves have plotted for your life.
Sir William.—I thank you for your service; take this
    purse.
    Be ready; in two days you may be sent
    With letters to the Council. Go, and refresh you.
                •   [*Exit* LAWYER.
    Why, this is as I'd have it; such a scene,

The violence, the contempt a magistrate
Speaking by writ received, this laid before
The Privy Council, worded as I could word it,
Might seem a riot, or a treason.   No!
I would not take his life, but let him be
Prisoner in the keep of Edinburg ;   [venged
Then were this young snake tamed, I were re-
For that fierce contest, searching, dangerous,
That maze of lawsuit that his father led me.
This youth must be attainted—might he not
Wrest from me all I've gained? this castle, land?—
Could not changed ministers make confiscate ?
Would he were limited to ten square feet,
That I might hold these miles with safety !

Enter LADY ASHTON.

Lady A.—So busy, Sir William ?

Sir William.—I am, and over urgent business.

Lady A.—But I come on urgent business too. Attend!—

Sir W.—Another time !

Lady A.—You shall hear me now, or never hear what
concerns your daughter's welfare at all.

Sir W.—What, Lucy's?   Well, let me hear it.

Lady A.—She is arrived at a marriageable age, William.
Have you any reasonable suitor to propose ?

Sir W.—I have not.   Lucy is free to choose.

Lady A.—It remains with me as usual to guard the
honour of our family.   Lucy is not to choose for
herself.   I have already chosen for her.

Sir W.—Whom ?

Lady A.—Mr. Hayston, the Laird of Girnington.

Sir W.—The man who has just come into the property of Lady Girnington?

Lady A.—The same: he is a rich man and a man of influence.

Sir W.—Well, we'll think it over.

Lady A.—The carriage is waiting. We had better go together and call on the new Laird.

[*Exeunt.*

END OF ACT I.

ACT II. SCENE I.

THE CAVE OF DESPAIR, 'FAR UNDERNEATH A CRAGGY CLIFF.'

DESPAIR *on a rocky throne. Around him, leaning against old stocks and stubs of trees, a council consisting of* REVENGE, SPITE, MURDER, *and the* SEVEN DEADLY SINS.

Sloth.—Why am I hurried here I fain would know,
    By spirits powerfuller than myself?   Why placed
    Amidst hard stones and stocks in this bleak cave,
    I that lie snug and feast among the rich ?—
    Curse on you all for this long speech, talk you !
Lust.—Ay, let us finish and return to earth,
    Where brother Sloth provides me work in plenty.
    I fain would triumph never ceasingly,
    Run like a fire through blood to the eyes, or lurk
    A maddening serpent, as I chance to find
    Together or singly all men.
Spite.—   Are there none
    To sway as evil spirits but yourselves ?
    Have you been aided, being witless both ?
    And shall you not advise with nobler spirits,

How to subdue the greater ones, not sluggards,
And shame-lost ere you meet them, earthly
   creatures ?
Will you not listen and applaud ?
Wrath.—   Wranglers, go !—
  Is this the talk we're met for ?   Speak, Despair ;
  If not I'll here defy all laws and go.
Murder.—And I too—lo ! the blood on this knife's dry.
Despair.—You bluster louder than my music sounds.
  The screech-owl and the wailing wind this cave
  Pierce both by night and day ;—and I must miss
    them !
  Now hear what's brought us.
Revenge.—Fellow-accursed, I got this summons for ye,
  That ye might hail me victor and rejoice,
  Applauding and conceiving all my triumph,
  Then that ye might devise how ye could share,
  Partaking in this triumph, making not
  Mine by a jot the less but yours as great.
  By certain oaths, and frowns, and pangs of spirit
  Which we have senses for, each for his own—
  You, brother Murder, for much kindred ones ;
  By certain lures, I say, which the earth betwixt us
  Could not prevent, in full flight to me came
  Bidding to be present, and to ply my darts,
  Leaving them wingéd on the air about him,
  Or to breathe myself upon the air he breathed.
  This ' he ' it was my chief delight to watch,
  Till Heaven's king bade his soul depart. In death

I mustered all my arts, my courage, power.
I saw him as in a phial to his son
That poison hand I had stored within his heart ;
This son now has the precious stock engrafted
Upon his vigorous root, and as I hope
Years and my skill shall make it bear more fruit.
This is my tale.   I share my triumph with you,
Yet lessen nothing of it.   Can your wisdoms,
Each in his proper sphere, devise if aught
Your several labours may effect for you.
I can but see my own ; but you may share,
And not touch mine, taking the spoil that's
    yours.
Pride.—I triumph too in him as much as you,
And owe you nothing for this confidence.
Revenge.—But others, cousin, I vouchsafed this to.
Pride.—I answered as the chief of all here present.
Spite.—Why then are you not throned and president ?
Murder.—I know not whom you speak of.   Who is he ?
Envy.   }
Gluttony.   }   Who is he ?   We can never guess.
Covetousness.—I've met you on the threshold of a heart
Where I am lord.   Is that your ' he,' Revenge ?
Revenge.—With him I have faint power ; but he I
    spoke of
Acknowledges no sway of yours in thought.
Despair.—I know him not ; we none of us have
    summons.
Therefore, Revenge, reveal his name and place.

'Twill be for us the toilsome conflict only ;
No easy victory as it was with you.

Revenge.—His name's Lord Ravenswood ; the victim
whom
I urge him still against is the Lord Keeper ;
So is he called by those in the East Lothian ;
He holds the castle and its territory
That was the Ravenswoods' for centuries ;
He has a wife and daughter nearly woman—
All this I say to whet your wit and purpose.
You who could not approach Lord Ravenswood,
Can you find access to this family ?

Envy.—You spoke of ' he '; but that Lord Keeper's wife
I rule as you Lord Ravenswood.

Wrath.—   And I
As much as you !   [*To* ENVY.

Gluttony.—   I rule her son and servants !

Lust.—Envy has bid me look towards her daughter.
I've looked far off ; the Holy Spirit guards her.
I should be wounded by his sword, one step
Approaching nearer.

Spite.—   Poor foolish minx, I've hummed
Into her ear to help you, tunes of free songs ;
And she has answered innocently, singing
Words that you might have—

Lust.—   Might have what done to ?
How could I taint words more she would have left,
If once she had known them ?

Wrath.—   Choke yourself, Spite !

Have any of us power, or words or actions to
Put to the tongue or hand of any ?
Despair.—Have we not power, then, where God's spirit
    reigns not
To whisper ? to come on with the scowling rack ?
In moaning wind to utter it ? can we not
Prompt when a mortal's weak ? can you not,
    Wrath,
Follow each wrong with oath or wicked pledge ?
And, if your whisper groaned with a branch or
    hissed
With flood, was this not if he spoke it placed
Upon his tongue ?—you, Murder, can show knives
That else would lie dull, glittering, or in water
Spread a taste speaking of fell poison ; so, you,
    Lust,
Can wait for banquets to make fleshly-minded,
Then make flesh shine, eyes sparkle (what more
    easy ?)
Before the swimming eyes.   Come, Spirits,
    rouse ye !
Answer your powers, make greater your great
    names.
Ye've heard what dear Revenge has nobly told ye,
All for your benefits.   It remains you labour,
Each in his sphere employing perfect skill.
Profess and demonstrate your might as spirits !
As sleepless, inextinguishable sovereignties !
Opposed to puny mortals, strong alone

In their Creator's aid, that aid themselves
So oft refusing, oftener scorning given.
Now vanish earthwards ; here let darkness reign ;
Your bright effulgent presences withdraw,
And thunderous speech that awes my winds to
    silence !
They all vanish, and the cave becomes dark and silent.

SCENE II.

A WOODLAND SCENE.   ON A SEAT UNDER A TREE.

SIR WILLIAM ASHTON—LUCY ASHTON.

Sir William.—To you, child, life has been as a sunny
    wood,
As pure and sweet, the sorrows waving shadows,
The mystery as a peeping sky through foliage.
Would it could be so ever, that you could bring
Still, as you now bring to my wintry mind,
A summer in your breath, and eye, and step !
Ah ! but as seasons change, so years will change,
Making me sadder, taking my fairy from me.
Why lo, she hears me not ; my age is tedious.
I'll make her spirits answer cheerfulness ;

They are deaf to spleen—Lucy, what find you
  there ?

Lucy.—Dear father, you were smiling as you talked,
  And my thoughts strayed from wilful happiness.
  Now speak again your thoughts !

Sir William.—   They were too sad.
  You caught the smile that mocked them, not the
    sadness.
  Your sweet hive keep the honey ! Give me some.
  What were you watching, or what thinking of,
  Looking on nothing ?

Lucy.—   Gladly I'll tell you. 'Twas
  This pretty comedy, upon a stage
  Of mossy green, a single little actor
  Frisking upon it, lighted by darting sunbeams.
  One second-space upon that root was poised,
  After his downward run, a little squirrel,
  Who then sprang on the turf, light as a leaf
  That a breeze has eddied, where his eye had seen
  One precious nut, that nimble little hands
  Caught and held up to his mouth, o'er which his
    eyes
  Brightened, and that thick feathery grace of tail
  Waved triumph. 'Twas too brief; for lo, a fern
  Bowed lower by the wind, sent shadows o'er him;
  At this, the pretty scared thing dropped his prize,
  And scampered to a branch—a watch-tower
    whence,
  No enemy seen, he soon returns, or nearly ;

For ere he reached it your foot crushed a twig ;
Now seeing me too move he's vanished, perhaps
To where his woody cave lies far above us.

Sir William.—From which my wisdom gleans that
 smallest things,
Most innocent and seemingly most free,
Are yet debarred not shadows real to them.
So must it be with all, my daughter.

Lucy.—   Yes
 I would we two could live together here !
For here you smile, dear father, as you smile not
Within your lordly castle ; would we were
Cottagers here like your mere servants are,
Yet with our minds not sordid, but quite free ;
And glad as these summer guests, the birds and
 bees.   [pain

Sir William.—This is a dream, no life on earth, where
And care must be within, if all without
Is golden happiness ; as winter comes,
That changes all this glory, so come moods,
Treacherous as storms on cedared ocean isles ;
So doubts, remorse, reproaches, pangs (if none
For the past as keen for the future years)
Will gloom and toss our minds, that now are
 lakes,
Mirrors for every leaf and lapping gently
A little boat, and now are blackened gulfs
Hurrying their foam and all that trust them on
 them.

Lucy.—Look, sir, you've called down judgment—see
　　there peeps,
No more an innocent squirrel ; 'tis a bull,
He seems scarce tame.

Sir William.—　　　　　Come, Lucy, we'll return ;
The creature sees us not ; we need not fear it.

　　　　　　　　　　　　　　　　[*Exeunt.*

　　　　　Enter LORD RAVENSWOOD.

Ravenswood.—I range these coverts a mere fugitive,
And tread another's lands that should be mine.
All this wide champaign and this wood that
　　skirts it,
With more beyond the castle and around it,
All were my father's, and his father's father's.
Here have they chased with hounds and merry
　　horn,
Leapt with their steeds, or reined them 'mid these
　　glades,
And spread the hunter's feast.　I wander here
With less share of these than their ghost might
　　claim,
And am a weak unmanly thing, denied
The sport that nerved them for exploits of war,
And braced their sinews till more gloriously
They swung the battle-sword.　I will not bear it.
If here I may not hunt, I too can fight,
And win perhaps glory.　I will sail for France.
But first I will confront this cunning wretch,
Reproach him with his knavery, call the curse

Which the innocent base-defrauded may call down.
He shall be plainly shown his villany.
Who knows ! some keen remorse may visit him,
And be my slow avenger when I'm gone.
Hold ! who are walking there ?—'tis he, and with
   him,
His innocent daughter—she's his guardian angel,
And has averted for this day my curses.
Why have they stopped, what holds them ?   Oh,
   is't so ?

     RAVENSWOOD *levels his gun and fires.*

'Twas timed to but one second, the fell brute
In but a second had been trampling them
Fallen beneath his horns.   See, she has fainted !
I'll go to help that enemy.   [*Exit.*

Enter HOPE, FAITH, TEMPERANCE, *with attendant*
     FAIRIES.

Hope.—Dear sisters, peace may yet be born and live
Between these mortals angered by bitter loss,
And gain as bitter, of dull earth-possessions,
Of land and wealth that brings no store to the
   soul.
How all the gladder faculties of mind   [power !
Are clogged and droop with weight of vainest
Ev'n these, so nearly dead, I can inspire,
And with sky-brightness cheer death-clouding
   eyes.
Yea, sensual minds I prompt to taste in heaven
The joys of a spirit.

Temperance.—   But not on earth to know them,
Or breathe the airs of paradise as those
Who hate and wander far from pleasure's bowers.
Rapt are their souls, etherealised their bodies
Who purge off grossness by strict abstinence.
They here have visions with unclouded eyes,
Of glory more than earth's—of beauty greater
Than human face may glow with; even here
The music that enchants their inner sense
Is what their life still moves to, sweeter strains,
And more subduing to calm holiness,
Than any born of art, or nature-prompted
In fragrant woods as these.

Faith.—   This happy chance,
If it should bring pure thought to follow where
Before was passion and anger, then may grow
The glad assurance of sweet recompense,
And happy long eternity hereafter;
Where care and pain attended ease will come
To life not passion-troubled.   What far greater
Than frank and hopeful pureness will crown life,
Or fresh delight of young simplicity
Untouched by chill experience !   To untempted
And abstinence-true mortals, should the trust
In mighty Powers and Him, the chief one, come;
Then they have here a glad immortal's joy,
And touch and converse with immortal friends
Unseen and heard not—angels that on wings
O'ershadow, or in skies far distant sing.

FAIRIES *sing.*

We the spirits of the earth,
    Of its meadows, of its fountains,
Love the summer, greet its mirth
    In the field and on the mountains.

Where we come the zephyrs blow,
    When we smile the grass is greener,
When we sing streams murmuring flow,
    And the strife of bird is keener.

Love and joy so mingling play
    In our happy songs and faces,
That no mortal wit could say
    Which more, heart or sunshine graces.

With the night no sleep benumbs,
    Then the moon or glow-worm lightens,
Or we wander, fancy comes
    To the room a red hearth brightens.

If pure, happy man or maid,
    If sweet childhood sends us greeting,
From afar where we have strayed
    Come we with fair pleasures meeting.

Or a flower we wave to them,
    Or bird-warbling sweetly waken,
Or make tremble on a stem
    Dew that sunshine has o'ertaken.

Would we had some gifts for you,
Mighty angel-powers descended.
Both dear love and service true
In our fairy song is blended.

[Exeunt.

END OF ACT II.

ACT III. SCENE I.

LONDON : A ROOM IN COLONEL DOUGLAS ASHTON'S
HOUSE.

COLONEL *and* SERVANT.

Colonel.—Here are the letters ; this small one to Lady
Fairleigh, that sealed one to Captain Craigengelt.

Servant.—'Tis not addressed so, Colonel.

Colonel.—No, blockhead ; he's to deliver it.

Servant.—I understand your honour. 'Twill burn
our fingers taking it ; he's dead as soon as he
gets it.

Colonel.—He is, Johnson, if my sword answers my
hand.

Servant.—May we not give it him on a sword, Colonel ?
I am half afraid to touch it.

Colonel.—The letter it goes with will cool it, that is as
sweet as the other's bitter.

Servant.—I warrant it, sir ; and let me remind you I
told you of her first and found her nest.

Colonel.—Your duty, Johnson ; do the like again. Go
now, my wife comes home presently—let her not
see those letters.

Servant.—Tut, Colonel. I am secret and faithful, wise and cunning, quiet or loud, in any matter you choose to employ me, so long as I can lose money at play and drink wine at table.

[*Exit.*

Colonel.—Which two vices will always keep you my servant, friend. I could make your life miserable at a moment's notice, and therefore you must keep my pleasures going every hour. Ha ! this is a merry life enough. I challenge the husband and make love to his wife. What did he say in the House? I forget ; but I know I taunted him into giving me the lie. Hurrah for politics ! My dear lady mother will fill my purse as long as I support her party, and this means sword-practice and love-making. Ha! who's this? my wife's step. Why, plague on it ! my mother was to be here first and take her away. I shall now have to listen to her love-making, it is usually complaint-making. What matter ! it will give zest to an evening with Lady Soft-eyes.

Enter Mrs. Douglas Ashton.

Dear Clara, are you ready ? My mother comes to take you presently.

Mrs. D.—I am ready, Douglas ; but I would say a word or two before I leave you.

Colonel.—Ay, ay, I understand. It is good-bye! Well, I must attend the House, Clara. Kiss me now.

Mrs. D.—So cold! So brief! Douglas, you were not so once.

Colonel.—I know it, dear. Good-bye!

Mrs. D.—Stay, hear me, Douglas. This coldness makes me suspect you.

Colonel.—I hoped to part with you peacefully, but you will not have it so.

Mrs. D.—Oh, Douglas, look to yourself for the blame. Be the man you were, the kind, faithful husband I knew you once.

Colonel.—And know me not now! Is that your meaning?

Mrs. D.—Does not your fierceness force it on me? No! I do not know it, but would that you ceased to make me think it!

Colonel.—Well, Clara, have done with these foolish fancies? You see they waste my time and make your cheek pale—leave them to poor starved lovers.

Mrs. D.—Promise me one thing, Douglas.

Colonel.—What is it?

Mrs. D.—To leave this wicked London and this whirl of politics as soon as you decently can, and to live on some small estate in the quiet country.

Colonel.—Impossible, Clara. This wicked city and this whirl of politics are my very life.

Mrs. D.—And they cost the life of me.

Colonel.—You may live away from both, as you already do from one.

Mrs. D.—But knowing you are here would bring them stifling round me if I were across the ocean.

Colonel.—No, no, dear. Try fresh air and forgetfulness. See, here is my mother at last.

Mrs. D. (aside).—What a final stab is that phrase, ' at last.'

Enter LADY ASHTON.

Colonel.—Mother, I give Clara into your charge. Keep her out of politics or I must leave them too.

Lady A.—No, Douglas ; you shall press on still, and to be quite free I will take charge of her. Our enemies think to muster strong this next session, and our poor lord in Scotland may hold up his head. This is the dream of some.

Colonel.—And what is the reality, Lady Schemer ?

Lady A.—The reality is that we may drive him off the perch he has left to him, and may include his Wolf's Crag in our estate.

Colonel.—That would be pressing this lean bird too far.

Lady A.—Not if the creature has a beak and claws whetted by revenge, and a title, forsooth, greater than ours. Let him have no land or stone in Scotland and Scotland will soon hear no more of his title.

Colonel.—Of his title-deeds !

Lady A.—Have done jesting, Douglas, and take example less from your father than from me.

Mrs. D.—Are these his jests, Lady Ashton? He never jests now as he used to.

Lady A.—Yet you make yourself his jest by complaining of this. Come, dear, your company will make him a fool. Learn to esteem a husband for being serious, especially at such a time as this. Be thankful you have not a husband who can only learn to jest worse and worse.

Mrs. D.—I would laugh at his worst.

Lady A.—Come, come, you are now a fool in earnest. I see Douglas smiles. It is time you left him. Douglas, do you forget the House meets in ten minutes?

Colonel.—I had, indeed.

[*Going.*

Mrs. D.—Stop, you are forgetting to say good-bye.

Lady A.—Let him go, Clara. Why, that was happily forgotten when such pressing business urges. Go, Douglas, we follow you out.

[*Exeunt.*

———

SCENE II.

GARDEN IN FRONT OF OLD ALICE'S COTTAGE.

LORD RAVENSWOOD—LUCY ASHTON.

Ravenswood.—Call to her, Lucy. Let her come to meet us.

Let not our ent'ring startle timid age.

Lucy.—Nay, let us wait her leisure; 'tis the hour
    She paces round these favourite paths and touches
    Here perhaps or there a flower.
Ravenswood.—   She is guided
    In all her actions by some inner sense.
    I've talked with her, and she has gestured
        towards me,
    Answering my gestures like an orator
    That eyes his adversary.
Lucy.—   In the past she lives.
    Would she could cast our future for us: tell us
    Whether indeed this feud might end for ever—
    We be its healers.   Ah, me!
Ravenswood.—   Why that deep sigh, dearest?
Lucy.—Could we but in a little home like this,
    'Midst blossoming roses, live thus in a wood
    Quiet as this!—how often would my singing
    Float from the windows, mingling with the birds'.
    What sweetness were within, what peace without!
    Think of our summers in such paths as these
    Stepping together with light steps, encircled
    With happy arms; then plucking autumn fruits
    Or greeting with like smiles spring's blossomings.
    Think in grim winter what warm gentleness
    Would from our hearth shine on all faces round.
    Ah! pomp may come, and wealth may find us
        happy,
    Yet not so sweetly happy.
Ravenswood.—Holy simplicity has made you, dearest,

A fount of quiet sunshine ; your child's heart
Speaks from your eyes calmly and sweetly too.
Nay, I repeat but what their sweetness taught me.
I could not hate an enemy like you ;
And that revenge bequeathed to me with curses,
I found die in me like ill ghosts at dawn.
You were the dawn that broke the clouds which
    brooded
So long upon our house. Then, dear, be happy,
As I am happy, feeling peace within me,
And sunshine in my breast where surged dark
    tumults.
Talk you of peace and happiness as but
Guests of sweet cottages as this ? Then know
That they may visit palaces, that pomp
May be sweetly borne, borne with humility ;
Wealth may be deemed a discipline, and bowed to
Lowly by the holder as to trial sent.
Does peace and happiness here reign where roses
Cling in embrace and birds sing cheerfully ?
It is the calm of death—here a poor blind one
Is slowly deathwards creeping ; 'tis an avenue
Where one with funeral pace is tottering to
Her grave.

Lucy.—   Dear Edgar, what a gloom of thoughts !
Your words have brought on darkness. How I
    shudder !
Surely this is not summer, nor these flowers
Live here sweet lives.

Ravenswood.—   Lucy, I cannot cheer you,
Thinking too much how future woes may sadden,
Alas! may separate.   Oh, let this thought
    strengthen,
Know that I'm ever your dear love to shield you;
Though absent, think you ever have the love
That stronger is than death—how then can
    foes ?—
Let not ev'n spiritual terrors quell your mind.

*Lucy.—*Edgar, you catch the gloomy tone and sad-
    ness
With which old Alice hints presentiments.
I fear not change in you, dear ; fear in me
No change that terrors, either foes or spirits,
Could awe and strike with ; but why talk of such ?
Does not my father see and countenance
All that has passed between our hearts of love?

*Ravenswood.—*Dear Lucy, come; we'll use a rustic
    pledge—
I break this gold in two, take you the half of it,
And swear to keep it.

Lucy.—   This I take to wear
Next to my heart, nor part from it till you
Join that half to it, when this contract's void.
I swear by heaven to do this !

Ravenswood.—   And I, too,
Will keep this next my heart, nor take it thence
To lose it till you join your half to it.
I swear by heaven to do't !

Enter O̓LD ALICE.

Alice.—What voices here ? What words are those ye
utter ?

Lucy —We are friends, that visit you.

Alice.— And he ?

Lucy.—A friend of mine and yours.

Alice.— Of mine, not yours!

Ravenswood.—Her friend, your friend, her dearest,
Alice, friend.

Alice.—Ha, but now speak ! how comes this, Ravenswood
And Ashton—such two, friends ?

Lucy.— Yes, to my father ;
He's staying in our castle, where my father
Offers him kindness, gives him with his hand
Friendship to last for life.

Alice.— And you, my lord ?

Ravenswood.—I answer courtesy like his as kindly,
And will not lengthen this long feud. A curse
Cannot be still bequeathed, as I was prompted
To take it and deliver it. I say
That Christian charity prohibits this,
And louder calls for obedience.

Alice.— Will this save
You from a death of ignominy—her
From worse than death, then death to follow this ?
What fatal days, and weeping trains !—poor dame !
So haughty, you shall bend. But you, Sir
William,

Oh, you shall be a willow crushed by storms,
Rooted up, plunged in the eddying stream, down
   hurled !
Alas ! for youth, for beauty blasted so !
Lucy.—Poor Alice, age is making wreck of thoughts,
And sending thick dark fancies to your brain.
What visions are these ?—can you see the sky,
That you so stare upon it ?
Alice.—   Ay, so heaven wills !
Tell me, do I now look upon bright skies,
Or is night there ?
Lucy.—   To your sealed eyes 'tis night.
May I guide you, Alice ; talk more cheerfully.
Come, let me read to you.
Alice.—   I once could see,
And till this hour I could look up and tell
Where the sun stood, if skies were summer skies,
And how much after dawn, what hours were left.
But now 'tis night. Will Lucy Ashton guide me ?
Lucy.—I will right gladly in the paths you know.
I've seen you surely treading them.
Alice.—But now I know them not. How light your
   step is !
Dear child, your step's still light.
Lucy.—How her thoughts wander ! how she weakens
   too !
Wait not, dear Edgar, I shall stay with her.
Alice.—Ay, let him go ; come in, and shut my door.
                     [*Exit with* LUCY.

Ravenswood.—I like not words so ominous and boding.
　　She speaks with raven voice, and this chimes sadly
　　With thoughts I cannot stifle.　I have flung
　　All that revenge my father deemed so just—
　　And who knows 'tis not just ?—this father's kindness,
　　How if it be but smooth hypocrisy ?
　　Her mother's mood, will that be kindness or
　　A tiger-hate ?　That way the whisperings
　　Share hard and smooth between them.　And this fairy,
　　Is she a strength and noble spirit I
　　May grow and strengthen near and nobly wing with
　　While life shall last ?　Her gentle beauty is,
　　Yea, and her sweet soft temper, rest and peace ;
　　Obedience too, and concord, that will shine
　　As light in a cloud within our earthly home.
　　Enough ! no more I crave ; how this o'erbuys
　　My paltry vengeance with the pride of them
　　Who bade me keep it !　Even yet I fear,
　　By how much love I bear her gentleness,
　　That dear obedience will be weak surrender
　　And quailing in the face of enmity,
　　Quelling her love as thunder stills the birds.

P

SCENE III.

LONDON: CAPTAIN CRAIGENGELT'S CHAMBERS.

SQUIRE HAYSTON—CRAIGENGELT.

Hayston.—And you're his second, Cragie?

Craigengelt.—In this duel, as in the other three.

Hayston.—Then he shall not have you for the fifth; for I'll have you myself.

Craigengelt.—I'll second both. It is sport I like. I bet against my man, and if he lives he pays it.

Hayston.—And, because fortune never gave a favour to such a scoundrel as yourself, the man you second always does live.

Craigengelt.—Laird Hayston, I can take affront from you because of your new importance.

Hayston.—And you could take affront before because of your own importance—to your country.

Craigengelt.—Well, well, we know each other and can joke.

Hayston.—But I'm not inclined to joke. I want you to be my second against Colonel Ashton.

Craigengelt.—Have a care, Laird; he is the devil at a home-thrust!

Hayston.—Do you think I am a coward? What do I care for his home-thrusts. Listen to my grievance.

Craigengelt.—Ay, what has he done?

Hayston.—He has done nothing. It is the family have insulted me. You remember Lady Ashton put her daughter Lucy into my head, that I asked her permission to court Lucy, and obtained it. Now, listen what follows! I go to the castle to see the girl and find an accepted suitor there.

Craigengelt.—How, an accepted suitor?

Hayston.—Accepted by the father. It was Lord Edgar Ravenswood. He is at this moment staying in the house. The old gentleman preached me a sermon on the subject of forgiveness of injuries and the advantages of a close alliance.

Craigengelt.—What!—said his daughter was to marry Ravenswood?

Hayston.—Not exactly that, but he said as much as showed he was only waiting for one of them to ask him.

Craigengelt.—And what said Miss Lucy?

Hayston.—Oh, she sees nothing and is as simple as a child. If the girl herself favoured him I would let her go, and be hanged! But what galls me is that these deceitful parents should trifle with me so.

Craigengelt.—Do you think Lady Ashton would preach forgiveness and close union?

Hayston.—I fancy the devil would show his cloven foot if that was tried.

Craigengelt.—I know she hates Ravenswood. We all know her will is Sir William's too ; you say the parents, yet name but him—rather name her and you name the parents.

Hayston.—But what shall I do ?

Craigengelt.—Send me to her instead of to Colonel Douglas, and you will find yourself escorting her to Scotland to-morrow.

Hayston.—Go, my dear boy !—but do the escorting for me too. I'll go to Scotland and get the manor in order for you.

Craigengelt.—For the bride, Laird, for the bride !

[*Exeunt.*

SCENE IV.

A FOUNTAIN-SIDE ON THE ASHTON ESTATE.

Enter PEACE, SIMPLICITY, PURITY—PEACE *in white flowing robes,* SIMPLICITY *in a sky-blue girdled robe,* PURITY *in a lustrous silver-shining mantle.*

From the other side enter COURAGE *and* HONOUR, *each in purple military cloak, with helmet in his hand and sandals on his feet.*

Peace.—Assure us, mighty princes, that he too,
    As she is changed, changes to that blest mood
    When concord's music breathing from far skies

Is heard above the tumult of this earth,
With all its envies, strifes, and jealousies ;
That not a thought disturbs save thought of good.
Is he within my kingdom ? may they live
Together, serving me and honouring these
My sisters ?
Honour.—   Yes, great queen, we gladly came,
Hearing your joyful summons, since we come
To tell that he who serves us faithfully,
Who was in bitter hatred, now has eyes
That kindly, lovingly meet those he shunned,
That light and rainbow sheen now mingling play
Where lightnings glittered, yet that nothing's
      lost
Which it became his spirit nobly keep.
Courage.—He would be still adventurous, and risk
Limbs as before in fight—yea, and the toil,
The cares of life that shame a noble pride
He would endure, still graced with constancy,
But that a sweeter lot rewards him.
Purity.—Our thanks to you, sirs, that your vigilance
Has awed pretenders who had used your names
To dim his youth's frail judgment, hiding from
      him
Paths that led on to happiness as rare
As they were faint. But what could vision quicken,
And cloudy error chase from his clear mind,
If not strong purpose and integrity
Prompted by you ?—this made sight eagle-eyed,

And joined a dove-like wisdom to it; this
Has crowned him great successor to the house
Whose fame he was to win back by revenge,
Heaping on loss disgrace—so ran the curse.
Now, see what grace and glory no revenge,
And more, ev'n reconciling love can give!
Oh, to receive the charge of vengeful hate
Was noble, to translate it thus to love
Is nobler still.   How youth may sometimes shine
With truth and beauty soul-born, while the sire
Counsels in madness scorning to look within!
Had this youth not obeyed still conscience, but
The shout of his raged father, then this house
Had with its losses fallen, that now stands
Stately on losses smiling.

Simplicity.—Henceforth   I   see   my   favourite   child
        embraced
By love's arms and by glory's; hers will be
No shrinking love, nursed 'midst alarms and anger.
She has that crown of woman, holy love;
And he who loves, the sacred vows that bind them
Will call down praise upon her; these have built
A throne of justice and strong unity,
Whereon she shall sit cherishing dear love,
Dowered with all earthly blessings, dear to him,
And nearer heaven.

Peace.—Let chiefest joy be for this concord won,
That the stored fruits, and golden glory shed
From this rich horn will be poured out upon them.

Princes, you bring us joyful hope of this.
Now let us hover round invisible
Where these two beauteous mortals walk alone,
Or with embracing arms, and be we near them.
Their speech attuning, wakening sweet grace,
And making looks beam eloquence, each one's
Majestic sad or radiant; let them see
Beauty and pure solemnity and love
With each shy glance, then utter gentle words
Of soft air-music, solemn as that or glad.

The scene closes.

END OF ACT III.

ACT IV. SCENE I.

A ROOM IN THE CASTLE.

SIR WILLIAM ASHTON—LADY ASHTON.

Sir William.—What, bid him go!—turned him out with insult? my guest!—why is this?

Lady Ashton.—To save us from worse ruin. What have you done!—taken a serpent to your breast —to her breast, perhaps—then, ask you why I fling it away?

Sir William.—Who is a serpent?

Lady Ashton.—Lord Ravenswood! I'll show you why. He comes to creep into our daughter's affections; to win some of our wealth, that he may spend it as wickedly and as foolishly as his fathers have spent money; to flaunt his empty title in our eyes; to scorn us all, if his cunning should succeed. Is this the creature you foster?

Sir William.—And how if he be not so penniless and mean? how if his party do not win him back some of the estate? Lord Athole, his friend here, will tell you what a chance he has. Is it not wise then to keep friends with him? Would a match with Lucy be so ridiculous if he should regain more than half possession?

Lady Ashton.—Lord Athole told you this! I have been in London six months, watching the turns of fortune, talking with ministers, and with the Duchess of Marlborough herself. This is mere invention of Lord Athole's. It is no doubt to do a kindness for his friend. But we are to think if this would be a kindness for ourselves.

Sir William.—It is, if this is true.

Lady Ashton.—It is the wildest of untruths; but granting this may be, would you see calmly this last rag of nobility and poor proud rake joined to our house, and one of our family?

Sir William.—I find him peaceable and well behaved. I don't know that he is addicted to vice.

Lady Ashton.—You don't know, and you won't know till it is too late, unless I stop it. But this is done. I sent him words that will chase him from here. I know how to lash his ridiculous pride.

Sir William.—Then it is too late! I can do nothing to keep up our character for hospitality and charity.

Lady Ashton.—And blind folly!—no!—But tell me now; is not the Laird Hayston everything you could wish for a son-in-law? His estate good, his person handsome, his character fair.

Sir William.—I know nothing against him. What are you going to do?

Lady Ashton.—Leave all to me. Lucy shall be pressed to name the wedding-day in all due time. At

present, owing to your weakness, that person has
got some influence over her.

Sir William.—If he has won her heart, she shall
marry no one else, though she does not marry
him.

Lady Ashton.—I said nothing about heart. I think I
understand my daughter. No, no, it is a trifling
sentiment that will soon leave her memory.

Sir William.—I never encouraged her to feel more, or
indeed to be anything but friendly to Lord
Ravenswood.

Lady Ashton.—No great mischief is done yet; and if
you will leave Lucy to me all will be well.

Sir William.—I do, with all my heart—these affairs of
love I cannot have the patience to understand.

Lady Ashton.—Nor are they intended for a man's
understanding. They are a woman's concern,
and a mother's. Come, we must find our guest.
And listen with a deaf ear to the folly he talks
of his party and their prospects. Remember,
William, you have a listener of councillors and a
receiver of private news in me too.

[*Exeunt.*

SCENE II.

HADES.

At a cloud-built table with imaginary viands on it, the spirits of LORD RAVENSWOOD *and several ancestors; also, the spirits* REVENGE, WRATH, *and* LUST. CHARON *presides.*

Lord Ravenswood.—Tell me again—some spiteful spirit
    told me
  My son was making league and amity,
  Was breaking oaths to my death-bed.
Revenge.—   All is changed !
  I was quite dispossessed of mine and banned.
  Those glistering meek slaves to goodness, Peace,
  Simplicity, with Honour and the like,
  Hovered around my son and favourite;
  Taught him their looks and language; showed to
      him
  Visions of future bliss and paths I knew not.
  All was to be bright thought, and light should
      shine,
  Like that gleams from yon Heaven, round about
      him.
  I and my darkness were not once to gloom him.
At this moment the spirits of other ancestors, with an ANGEL, *approach the hall.*

Charon.—Stop, spirits.   Let me answer these who
    haunt us !

Angel.—Break up your cursed assembly.   Boast not
    here,

As if in Hell already, of great sin
That some unhappy spot of earth beholds.
Charon, I say, dismiss them ; touch this vision,
And let this table vanish, and these walls !

Charon.—Begone, these spirits have their liberty ;
I grant them this device, and hear their speeches.
They may not yet be tortured with good thoughts,
With fierce remorse from sight of naked ill
They did on earth, nor with reproaches keen,
When they shall see afar off blessèd spirits.
Begone, and torture not yourselves, you good,
And sorrowing ancestors—this is Hades ; 'tis
Nor Heaven nor Hell, and I am Hades' ruler.

                  [*They vanish.*

Revenge.—I say that all is changed !

Wrath.—   Bid vassal spirits
Chase, and with wickedest curses plague those
    spirits,
Who came to mock us.   Let not that angel stay
    here.
Charon, I say—dost hear me ?

Charon.—   Did'st hear me ?—
Art thou here master ? speak again advice
And insolent bidding, I will chase thee hence,
To wander lonely with but half-friend men !

Revenge.—Have pity, Charon; let our ears drink
   pleasure;
And give us all companionship awhile.

Charon.—Proceed! I'm peaceful to obedience.

Revenge.—I say that now most sweet confusion's near,
   The spirit Peace is weeping fled from him;
   Bloodshed may come, but death and foul disgrace
   Is near.

Lord Ravenswood.—Disgrace and death for which of
   them?

Revenge.—Death for your son; it cannot but be so,
   But he is one, be cheerful, they all die;
   All meet disgrace, and die, if not of grief,
   Of bitter shame. This must be so, if such
   The tide of passion and its height in two,
   At the least in two frail human hearts; they must
   Burst, and in bursting shatter kindred hearts.—
   Speak, Wrath, will this tide cease but with
   A riving of its channel? will it cease
   To seethe till swallowed by the gaping cleft
   Of earthquake-death?

Wrath.—   This is your wish.
   But I can see a heart, and have seen many,
   That burn with my flame unconsumed for a life,
   A life of generous measure; such is this one;
   Mine is a spirit of strength, as well as might.
   What tell you me of tides? I scorch, yet burn
      not.

   A spirit creeps to LUST *and whispers.*

Lust.—Spirits, I'll say my speech and leave ye ; lo !
    I've summons from the earth, where myriad
       sparks
    Should now be blown to flames.   I let them lie ;
    But now word comes they must be blown or
       perish.
    This, then, is my delight regarding these,
    That the pure love, which had so nearly triumphed
    Is now quite frustrate ; so the triumph's mine !
    That pure example had quite shamed my arts
    In many where I still may work at will.
    These I may still fail once to touch ; at least
    They will not thwart and vex me ; now I go;
    Make me not speak more ; I'm in haste to go.
Charon.—You have your liberty to pass these walls.
    Come not again, but on a like occasion !
Lust.—Gladly ! this fleshless place, spirits like these
      but cheer.

                                [*Exit.*

Revenge.—Well, spirits, brother Wrath disputes my
      triumph—
    See, we both triumph ; what can exceed success
    When partners and twin zeals each compass it !
    Each attain fullest ! drink, brother Wrath, to
      mine,
    I drink to your success, both being so sure.
Wrath.—Here, take my drink, and give me yours ; so,
      best,
    We mingle tempers.

*They drink fire, which courses through them ; the others
    shudder.*

Charon.—Enough of fiery drinks and speeches ! turn
    your eyes
Where milder sights and sounds may greet you.

*An army is seen marching to martial music, their
looks noble and defiant ; suddenly all the horrors of a
battle are seen, and the music changes to discord.*

*Children are playing in fields ; suddenly they are
grown men and women, drinking and wrangling in gaudy
tap-rooms.*

*An orator is stirring a crowd to patriotism ; suddenly
it is dark, he is taking a bribe with one hand, and un-
fastening the city gate with the other.*

*A preacher is seen exhorting a congregation to holi-
ness ; then they are seen to separate and speak poisonous
words, at which the hearers sicken ; they handle false
weights, bad books, &c., they are seen stealing opinions
from others, putting their hands into the hearts of others
and crushing out tender feelings ; selling the opinions
afterwards as their own.*

*Singers and musicians are seen to make people weep ;
a painter exhibits pictures, on which people gaze with
rapture ; a poet is reciting his verses to an enthusiastic
audience. Then loud thunder terrifies the audience listening
to music, which ceases in discord ; blinding dust enters the
eyes of the picture-viewers, and the colours are all defaced ;
the poet is mocked by an invisible speaker, who is heard
as distinctly as he is ; his audience look angrily at him,*

and, in going, pick up leaves of his book, which are
found to contain words of ribaldry, excellence, impurity,
and noble feeling all mingled together.

Lord Ravenswood.—What means this, Charon, tell us!
 What scenes, and crowds, and thoughts, have
  passed me ; yet all seems mingled.
 Less numerous than diverse!

Charon.—These walls I've skill to make reflect all rays
 Or mingle all ; this heaped variety
 Comes from the mingling of most diverse beams,
 More than can be on earth ; hence these were
  visions
 Earth cannot show ; and yet the types are there,
 But separate, never joined to write this language.
 These walls have focussed for us on that space
 The light of Heaven's pure shine, and glare of
  Hell.
 Hence were the scenes so blent, goodness and evil
 With such quick change supplanting each the
  other.
 It is a fable and a sport here ; but on earth
 This is a bitter truth. Spirits, I bid ye vanish!
 One touch of mine must now make all dissolve.
 I call ye not again nor serve your pleasure,
 Till spirits like these have need of you ; you come
 To Hades only bringers of joy—now vanish !

   The scene closes.

SCENE III.

A ROOM IN THE CASTLE.

LADY ASHTON—AILSIE GOURLAY.

Lady Ashton.—I say she's sick, but not so sick in
    fancy
As I would have her. Can you heal the one
And sway the other ?
Ailsie.—   Ay, madam, both.
She shall have fancies and be strong to fancy.
Lady Ashton.—You   know   the   legends, proverbs,
    prophecies,
That darken this name Ravenswood, and awe
From union, even friendship with them ?
Ailsie.—'Tis said they won estates, wealth, wives alike,
    By bloodshed, bold as robber chiefs, or treacherous.
The fifth of the line, the eighth, some few besides,
Have won fair high-born dames by influence
Peaceful and just ; but he, the fifth, accused
By her, poor proud one, of unfaithfulness,
Assembled on a night his paramours,
And while to music feasting with them, heard
His orders being obeyed, her soul sent forth
From an upper window, following her shrieks.
That eighth lord, strangled some say, poisoned
    others,

Q

His sweet wife of a year; she was livid found.
He heard her taunting him for love of gold;
When years had gone her spirit haunted him.
He died pursuing it, and sword in hand
Had leapt a precipice.

Lady Ashton.—   A cursèd race! you know
   Doubtless a prophecy or so as fatal?

Ailsie.—Ay, let none match with one of them; 'tis
      said,
   The last—and this may be the last—will woo,
   Not a fair bride, not a rich, no bonny bride,
   A dead bride to his arms! think of it fair ones.
   Poor murdered wives before have yet been wives;
   This last on the wedding night shall die.

Lady Ashton.—   Hush, hush!
   You comment much too fatally; you fright
   Me who am steel to fears—yet Lucy's stubborn
   It must be told, perhaps indirectly, yet
   Told her as she may know what mishap waits
   On any marrying with this fiendish race.
   I may call them such if what you say be true.

                Enter a SERVANT.

Servant.—Madam, you bade me bring all letters to you.
   Here's one was given me to give elsewhere.

Lady Ashton.—You do your duty; go, and keep watch
      still.
   If any negligence lets go by any
   That moment you're dismissed.

                        [*Exit* SERVANT.

Lady Ashton (*reading letter*).—I shall stay two
months—I then must go to France. But let
me hear from you, though I cannot see you.
The bearer of this is faithful to us, you can send
by·him.

(*Aside.*) So now we know your tactics, noble lord.
She shall not answer you, or she may write,
As she has written, never shall it reach you.

(*Aloud.*) You know your part, Dame Gourlay: when I
call
Come to my daughter's chamber. I must leave
you. [*Exit* LADY ASHTON.

Ailsie.—I would not second you so willingly,
Press on your daughter cruel fears like these,
Were I not, hated though I am, and praised
As you, great lady, may be, far your better
Where mother-feeling's talked of. Can I but
Make this weak thing, her daughter, weaker still.
Ev'n then Laird Hayston marries her, but she,
Her beauty gone with health and power of mind,
Will never rival my strong daughter's beauties;
My daughter's not enslaved or banished, keeping
Still her old place in this Laird Hayston's love—
He promised her 't should be so ; but this plan,
And my skill here, shall make that promise sure.
This is the worst—it may be he'll not wed her.
[*Exit.*

END OF ACT IV.

ACT V.   SCENE I.

CALAIS: A HILL-SIDE NEAR THE HARBOUR.

RAVENSWOOD.

Here let me rest and meditate—how soon
Wafted from Scotland I tread foreign shores!
Hail to thee, land dearer to me than mine !
Welcome, ye strangers, and your language to me.
But, O ye land of glory, welcome more !
Terror of battles, honour with death-wounds
    bought,
Thanks from the heart-sore and life-desperate for
Moments when life 'midst death blazes or dies too!
See, with this sword I'll teach my sinking heart
Strongly once more to beat, the smouldering fire
To brighten and flash forth from my eyes, or
    learn
What peace is with the honoured lying dead.
            Two French soldiers pass by.
1*st.*—Qui est ce monsieur-là ? mais qu'il est morne !
2*nd.*—C'est un diable anglais ; il est maintenant triste.
    Savez-vous pourquoi ?   Parce qu'il n'est pas ivre-
        mort.   [ivres.
    Tous les anglais sont tristes quand ils ne sont pas

1st.—Sans doute il médite de faire le suicide.

2nd.—Interromprons-nous ses méchantes méditations.
He! bon-jour, monsieur !

Ravenswood.—Good day, friends. Where is your
general ?

1st.—Allons-nous en ; il ne parle pas français.

2nd.—Adieu, monsieur.

[*Exeunt soldiers.*

Ravenswood.—I could not answer them ; my mother's
tongue
Clings to me ; ah ! and more than speech will
cling.
Can I forget her ? How my heart still yearns !
'Twas wicked folly to forsake revenge
So just, so solemnly inherited ;
But 'twas for her ; I had a heart for love ;
And she was beautiful and gentle too.
I felt in Paradise beneath her eyes,
And hearing music float from her dear lips
I've dreamt of golden peace that poets sing—
What Eden-bliss our innocence would know !
Was not the prophecy of gentle vows
A whispered fragrance round us ? Have I not
Symbols her fingers pledged with to all time ?
Has she not mine ? Oh, this was then a dream,
Or faith was her mere jest of acted faith.
She would not answer now, would meet my eyes
And wonder feign to see mine speak of love,
Whose cold heart felt it never—can this be ?

Was that look false, that trembling tear-drop false,
That tone which thrilled me, and those artless
    words,
Could they be false?   Oh, how if she poor deer,
Poor trembling fawn be pent in that retreat
By murderous threats without.   Her guardians are,
By cruel pride possessed, to devils turned ;
If feeling thwart it, kindness is nardness to them.
How can this poor soft soul of hers oppose
Devilry kindness-veiled—they force on her
This man their love for her, not her love, chooses.
Is not this murdering kindly, sweetly poisoning
Feeling and truth ?   O deadly foes to truth,
Hateful earth-dwellers to the pure good spirits
Who look on evil weeping that runs its course !
Yet stay, you Lucy tempt their wickedness ;
Did not my messages of agony
Spur you to one brief answer ?   Could you not
Face for one moment terror, to assure
Him who endured dark doubtful loneliness ?
Whose heart sank for your cheering; should I now
Speak to your face this charge, would not shame
    flush you ?
I cannot see this shame, thinking I see her,
Or give her face dishonour—who can tell ?
Some chance may have waylaid those messages,
My posts forgot their preciousness and gave not
The words I sent.   To hold such straws ! they
    were

Not one but fifty.   Yet I'll see this truth.
For one day, but for one, I will return,
And face the truth and her and all of hers,
Meeting their frowns, pierced by her words and
     looks ;
This done, I will return to serve despair,
Till welcome death shall hide me in the grave.
Enter the YOUNG CHEVALIER, CHARLES EDWARD
STUART, *an officer, a sergeant, and attendants.*
Officer.—Your Highness will embark a week from now ;
All is prepared ; the force we shall have with us
May laugh at Sir John Cope's.   But better still,
We may evade and pass him in the Lothians,
Going with unabated strength and forces,
Where no troops face us, south to England's heart.
Charles Edward.—Will Sir John Cope so suffer it ?
Officer.—   He is reported
An over-cautious leader, slow to move ;
His age would promise this.   Then, marking
     here,
This landing-place is near—Hist! who is yonder?
Speak to him, sergeant.
          RAVENSWOOD *comes forward.*
Charles Edward.—You have a sword, sir.   Are you
     serving us ?
We have strange faces hourly with us.   You are
     English.
Ravenswood.—A Scotchman, sir, who offers you his
     service.

Charles Edward.—My service is a desperate one ; you
know me ? [No,

Ravenswood.—I'm glad of it. I'm desperate too, sir.
I know you not.

Charles Edward.—You have a noble mien, a Scotchman ?—

Do you support or not the government ?

Ravenswood.—This government has robbed me and
my father,

And given estates of ours that centuries
Have still seen ours to its mere parasite.
We fought and lost our blood then lost our lands,
For what ? for thinking James, the crownéd king,
Should not submit to lose his lawful rights,
Divine and just. This cheating herd robbed him
And next robbed us—you see, sir, how I love
them.

Charles Edward.—A noble spirit! Come, sir, serve
with me,

And if success should bless me, I here promise
All those estates shall yet be yours—you wonder.
Come to that house and meet my friends, and
join us.

You shall hear gladly whom you serve, a prince
Who feels a pride in honouring such as you.

[*Exeunt.*

SCENE II.

HAYSTON—LUCY—LADY ASHTON.

Hayston.—You answer not, young lady, dear Miss
    Ashton.
    Pardon uncouthness that is honesty,
    Blunt, not untender, I would say I love,
    That I will love for life and learn each day
    To make you happier and to please you more.
    Can you accept and love me for this wish ?
    I cannot speak it better.
Lady Ashton.—   Lucy, dearest, speak ;
    This gentleman has offered you dear love ;
    He is our dear friend, mine, your father's too ;
    We've told him you have promised to be guided
    By what we wish for you ; and him we wish
    To be our son, your husband. Speak, my child,
    It is for you to answer.
Lucy.—   Madam, I promised this,
    This strict submission to you on condition,
    And not so as you say.
Lady Ashton.—   She means, Laird Hayston,
    The promise that intriguer got from her
    Is not renounced by him in answer to
    Requests she might recall it. Lucy, dear,
    His silence, whom you made this promise to

Written and signed, implies renouncement by
   him ;
You must not look for more ; he is ashamed
To answer openly ; but this is answer.

Lucy.—He may yet answer it; no time has passed
Sufficient for his answer.

Lady Ashton.   Not sufficient ?

Lucy.—No ; not by full a week since my last went.

Lady Ashton.—Have you then sent?

Lucy.—   Ay, madam, lately sent !

Lady Ashton.—What meant you, fool ; to drag
    dishonour on you ?
Undutiful, weak thing ! Now, dearest Lucy,
How could you do this ?

Hayston.—   Miss Ashton's right ;
And would I had delivered what she sent !
I would have fetched it from him.

Lady Ashton.—   Must we wait
Still till your messages are answeréd ?
Will you send new ones weekly, and refuse
To answer this approved friend ? Must his love
Be thrust aside while thus you trifle ?

Lucy.—   Spare me !
I will abide by this one, in one week,
By which time he could answer ; if he should not
I will obey you all.

Hayston.—   Nay, lady, though I long
To see you head my table with your graces,
I will postpone this longer than you say.

You act most honourably by this man,
And teach right feeling to us ; then be braver,
Demand more time.   I give you three, not one
    week ;
Reckon delays and accidents of travel
As all excuses for him ; but if then,
When thrice his shortest sending-time be passed,
You hear not from him, I shall claim you mine,
That day, St. Jude's day, you shall marry me.
Lucy—Sir, you are generous.   I have said I shall;
But till that day I must not speak to you,
And you will kindly cease to question me.
Hayston.—Till that day you are not to see or hear me.
I take my leave at once.   Till then, farewell,
Dear bride in prospect !
                            [*Kisses her, and going.*
Lady Ashton.—You'll speak with William, Laird,
    before you leave.
We must have conference on this together.
When next we meet 'twill be to sign and seal.
            [*Exeunt* HAYSTON *and* LADY ASHTON.
Lucy.—To sign and seal—to seal my coffin lid !
How am I pressed to this ! why, gallant lord,
Whose speech was music speaking of the theme
This boor in love untunes—why have you left
Her now so needing and so drooping for
One kind refreshing word, with desert-silence
To answer cries and listenings?   Oh, your beauty
And flow of musical speech is cruel art.

Your ancestors were lawless lovers to
Maiden and wife alike, you are their son.
You guess my sufferings, who knew my love—
Is this the love you spoke of strong as death ?
That knows my happiness is dying, brings
No life to raise it.   Oh, he mocks my love.
He sued for it, then scorned it, thinking love
That woman gave a ¦toy; so many think it;
Or spurred on by˜revenge he joyed to bruise it.
No, I'll not think so of him ; kind he is,
But to himself first; he would grieve to see,
And therefore looks not where pain answers him.
He fain would idly pass by pain in me
To rouse it in another.   'Tis man's pride.
Yea, taunt us, call our sex weak, worthless but
For your mere toy and pleasure, to be ta'en
Or left as chance comes, yet are women great,
And men the worthless ones if truth be worth.
Women are slow to vow, and pressed to vows
May break them ; but let her own heart propose
Gently its own true vow—on that rich soil
A sweet immortal flower braves all storms,
And blooms when storms are past in heaven, the
        home
Of that so precious birth—poor man and earth,
Unworthy ye to hold it !   Blush, O man,
Whose shows and lying words receive the love
Of her who undeceived yet loves ; your shows
Deceive poor artless maidens ; but their love

Humbles itself to love still ; then smile on.
It is your refuge from a death of shame
To say that our great love is but your due.

[*Exit.*

SCENE III.

THE SEMBLANCE OF A MOONLIT RUIN, BUILT OF

CLOUDS, AND OVER THE SPOT WHERE ASHTON

MANOR IS SITUATED.

TIME : MIDNIGHT FOLLOWING ST. JUDE'S DAY.

Standing in the arch 'of a window, DESTRUCTION.
Around him on the earthy stone-strewn floor, FAMINE,
DISCORD, MALICE, SWEARING, DRUNKENNESS, *these
all lighted by their own pallor. Swarming in the
darkness of the ruined aisles are myriad Lies, Envies,
False-accusings, Evil-thinkings, Hatreds, Uncleannesses,
Jealousies, Supplantings, Defamings.*

Destruction.—What, Malice ? say't again ! each detail
twice!
Thou sharpest-sighted spirit, feast our ears ;
What, he already stabbed !—to the heart did'st
say ?
Malice.—Lo, he has not had time to shriek before—

There now the breath's all from him, and the
    guests
Are still at the dance; all revel there, and here
All blood; but will she stab herself?—she laughs;
The murderess dances with a glee, the best—
The youngest, maddest at the ball seem tame.
Drunkenness.—There's drinking too! why all this talk
    of dance?—
I can see much deep drinking!
Famine.—   But no want—
Why was I summoned? 'tis to mock my power—
Discord.—Ay, let it perish, thou gaunt, emptying
    might!
Go, triumph not with us, or I will go,
Not to have my delight by selfish spleen
Tainted, or by your presence.
Destruction.—   Spirits, peace!
Hear wisdom first, then separate and rage.
Why am I here above? why have ye sworn
By that oath devils keep t'obey me here?
Not that I am your greater, though more wise,
None is more powerful of all of us,
But all are brothers.   Opportunity
May come to one or other—can it make
That one or other powerfuller? it comes
From me or him his neighbour; we do all
Give opportunity and take; and oft
The same is shared by two or all—what scorn,
And worthy puny man to raise dispute,

To call a brave work-fellow enemy,
Or think one selfish who his utmost zeal
Plying, at farthest limit of his sphere,
Admits the zeal and sphere of him who blames!
May not o'er this earth spot more spirits than one
Look in exultant joy ?   I've seen the fire
Ye've put in your heart's place, kindle and glow,
Your gleaming sights ye twice have changed to
    meteors,
To hear what Malice talked and see it too,
Quickened by him.   I too—ye saw me spread
Till all this arch was filled.   Now, Discord, speak,
How relish you this spectacle ?—see there !
They dance and she sits muttering—what peace !
But with the light, what terror !

Discord.—   King and brother,
I'm bound by oath to call you wise, yet now
I'll think myself yet wiser—what is this ?
Your opportunity not mine—see there !
It is all death, end both to strife and peace !—
While these fierce enemies and severed friends,
These lovers plagued and parted to my wish—
While both were well, not mad or dead, I say,
The sweetest tumult, jangling, tuneless noise,
Came to my ears, my eyes could see all thoughts
So mingled-maddening, yet not making mad ;
No reason or health-quailing, but as much
Of wretched variance as the heart of man,
Or that spot earth can hold.

Swearing.—   I so think,
And by hell's burning hold that all is here
Mere death, no lusty life of sin confused.
*Destruction.—*O weak short-sighted spirits, I can urge,
But not bring home true wisdom ; speak no more !
Ay, cast your lightnings feller than had tumbled
A towered height like this unruined, real.
Ye meet deservéd scorn.   I now command
Ye all with this pretence remove and sway
Above the spot where Ravenswood lies hid—
His horse, and gallantry, and beauty, all
Quenched in the shifting traceless sand.

                    They remove midway.

Malice.—   'Tis what ?
Not lightning now, no redness, purest light—
Tell me what's this, wise spirit ?—I must fly.
*Destruction.—*And I, too, all of us by some great power
Are now constrained ; the oath no longer binds.

    *The ruin changes to a sunlighted cathedral built of
clouds and over the same spot; from the windows,
which are painted, representations of saints and holy
forms seem to be invoking blessing.   Enter* TRUTH,
CONCORD, FAME, CHARITY.   *These all clothed as in
glistening sunny cloud.   Graces and cherubs fill the
aisles in white apparel.   Far up a kind of vista, St. Cecilia
is touching the notes of an organ, from which echoing
music rolls, and the cherubs sing reply.   Above all are
heard the speeches of the four, sounding trumpet-like
and melodious.*

Truth.—Look not below, sweet sisters, look above,
Upon that home to which they shall ascend
Whose love was purer than the earth can know—
As pure as zealous ; but that flame must be
Not held in earthly forms ; it cannot dwell
With breath and hours on earth, but must aspire.
How then could two such mingle ?   Both must
    flee,
But separate, to the blest abodes to clothe
Immortal spirit, spirit white and pure
In deathless free unhindering body ; none
Will there deny its great authority ;
None will pretend a bar to union there.
All wealth, and power, and might, and liberty,
Are there for each ; nor can between the two
Any weak jealousy or fearfulness,
One frail suspicion, or dark shadow come ;
For all is clear strong thought and feeling sure,
Gazing with undimmed eyes, unweighted heart,
A mind untrammeled, and untainted thought ;
The object looked on, loved, as beautiful,
As clear, and as delightful ; all is joy ;
The faithful lover and the loved one kiss
With thoughts as bright as faces ; each one sees
His, her idea reflected, summing all
In each sweet moment ; what he long has loved
In hope, and deeply hidden in his heart,
She offers him ; what she had whispering hid,
Not spoken and scarce thought, but trembling felt,

R

He gives eye, ear, and mind; their beauty is
Of soul and substance, grace in thought and look;
Their love is both an act and essence; now
A thrill of eloquence and now a mood.

Fame.—Upon the earth their memory shall live,
And add a fragrance to the sweetest thoughts;
Their story shall win entrance to the soul,
As melody sinks in attentive ears:
For not from anger shouting glory came
Their pleading to me, from no battle-field,
Where bravery had wrong and madness wed;
But from the depths of pure despairing hearts,
By worldly powers o'er-mastered, wrongly slain;
The might of circumstance, of custom's sway,
Wielded by servants of their tyranny.
The cry was to these noble ones a knell,
But not to honour, not to lofty praise;
The funeral chant of the mere body is
The song of triumph for their body's deed.
For all the good it sings of conquering souls;
For these of earthly deeds besides, that first
Their great souls though imprisoned prompted.

Charity.—Frailty has mingled with much nobleness,
Else had they not been human; but their names,
So much has sweet and noble grace come round
      them,
Shall waken no reproach. They have so lived
As to be mourned in death, to meet renown,
Which sweet and happy lives had missed; by death

They have been crowned to pattern noble life,
For death has shown their strength of love ; how
    strong
The sweetest, and the scorned by many, bond
Of simple pure souls may be—trust it, ye
Who cling yet trembling to it; and a thought
How strong, unworldly, unsucceeding love,
So checked and hindered, may be, must inspire
The sternest, most unwise. Now see, what
    power
In sweetness, that's no hardness, may be found !
See, from what earth is, losing such as these !
It would be poorer; I should mourn for it
That now has lost such ; but their memory
Will be a light and precious gift to shine,
To gild, to guide, and gladden as a sun.
Their lives on earth, though sweet and dear to
    earth,
Had been a humble cheering taper-light,
Sent from their homes on darkness ; now day-
    brightness,
They beam forth to us from the spirit world.
Concord.—Though strife may surge on earth, yet while
    a sky
Of calm blue ether stretches over it,
And while eternity is heir to time,
The rule unbroken will be peace, the end
A peace and rest. Some hours of every day,
Days of each year, and years of centuries,

By wars within, without, of thought and act,
Must still be troubled ; but the powers of wrath,
Of tumult and of trouble are of time ;
The spirits of great peace, of rest and joy,
Of love and amity, eternal.   Hence
The might their whispers give to minds like these.
The music they inspired was as a march
To which these hearts beat strongly, and could lift
Their spirit to this beauty; 'twas a march
And inspiration ; what they saw was great
And great their brave approach—that poise and
      height
They were down flung from ; they had else not
      been
Mortals upon this earth, nor now would soar
Above earth's highest to the height of heaven.

The music grows fainter and the vision gradually fades.

Printed by H. Blacklock & Co., Allen Street, Goswell Road, E.C.

ERRATA.

Page 73, *line* 13, *for* sin.   *read* sin,

,, 157,   ,,   21, ,, conveyed it.   ,, conveyed it